Tales from Dayrut

Tales from Dayrut

Mohamed Mustagab

Translated by
Humphrey Davies

The American University in Cairo Press
Cairo   New York

This paperback edition published in Egypt in 2015 by
The American University in Cairo Press
113 Sharia Kasr el Aini, Cairo, Egypt
420 Fifth Avenue, New York, NY 10018
www.aucpress.com

Dar el Kutub No. 22555/14
ISBN 978 977 416 707 2

Dar el Kutub Cataloging-in-Publication Data

Mustagab, Mohamed
    Tales From Dayrut / Mohamed Mustagab.—Cairo: The American
University in Cairo Press, 2015
        p.   cm.
        ISBN 978 977 416 707 2
        English Fiction

        823

1 2 3 4 5   19 18 17 16 15

Designed by Adam el Sehemy/AUC Press Design Center
Printed in Egypt

Contents

Dayrut al-Sharif

Hulagu

In the year nineteen twenty-something, my grandfather had left the city of Qus behind him and, with his traveling companions, penetrated deep into the belly of the mountains of the Eastern Desert. By the time the sun of the fifth day had staggered to the horizon in search of its extinction, the one path on which they had been proceeding had become a dozen paths, their eyes were darting in all directions, the camels were braying, their breath was coming in quivering gasps, and my grandfather whispered to the nearest of those with him, "We are lost." Unable to restrain himself, the man, embarrassingly, began to cry and his weeping spread to the others, who struck palm upon palm and passed many hours beseeching the Exalted to guide them aright, not least because they were on their way to visit His sacred house and the tomb of His noble prophet.

Over five more terrible days, the men grew exhausted, the camels flagged, and spirits weakened. All thought of the pilgrimage had been battered to shreds and one hope alone remained in their hearts—to find any path that would lead them to any place. My grandfather, however, was strong. He swore (to himself) that if he were saved from his present plight, he would build God a mosque unlike any in his village; and behold, some hours later, he found himself with his companions on the edges of none other than the city of Qus.

Scoundrels, and those who wish our family no good, say that my grandfather was the cause of what happened, that his attempted pilgrimage was not undertaken in good faith, for the sake of the Almighty, since he had intended when beside the Black Stone to seize that perfect, unique opportunity to call down God's wrath upon his enemies, et cetera, and that as a result, God had looked kindly upon the latter. One of them even slaughtered a bullock on the day my grandfather returned from his pilgrimage-less pilgrimage.

All that is known with certainty, however, is that on the morning of his return home my grandfather set off alone and wandered at length about the village. Eventually he stopped at the head of the triangle of mud formed by the canal and the entrance road and squatted there on his heels. He pondered the matter well and traced logarithmic lines. Then he stood up, threw his woolen wrap around his shoulders, and read the opening chapter of the Qur'an, to announce his intention to embark on the implementation of his decision, which was to build a mosque the like of which the village had never seen.

At a gathering aquiver with religious fervor he sat surrounded by his sons and certain of his allies. The month of Ba'una was almost upon them, the wheat was in the granaries, the sugarcane had gone to the factory, the sheep had been put out to graze on the fields, the men, at the season of the Nile's flood, were idle, and . . . . Did anyone have any specific objections to raise? Not one uttered a word, and each went his way, each feeling closer to God than ever before.

Within one month, the miry patch had been covered with earth and the building had risen to a meter's height. Then work stopped because of a common enough occurrence: my maternal aunt, on going to wake my grandfather, found that he had surrendered his soul to God.

Sometimes in matters of this sort God will send a man of strong personality, who gathers the others around him and completes what the great man, to whom the chance to prove his honest intentions (and discomfort his opponents) was not granted, had begun.

In view of the fact that no one of this description was to be found in my family, the meter-high walls were left standing sadly on the narrow triangle of land, the water welling up from below.

And given the uncertain nature of the religious conscience of the dogs of the village, some of them developed the habit during the winter that followed of passing by the walls to cock a hind leg and irrigate certain grasses that had crept out from between the courses of the bricks.

Nor was it long before lizards, yellow waters, and wasps' nests accumulated, the wasps making a low buzzing sound around the building that stirred fear in the hearts of the weak-spirited.

Now, I have an uncle on my father's side who was facing certain tribulations in life, having broken his right leg climbing the wall of a widow of conspicuous beauty while on a mission of whose details I am ignorant, thus rendering himself for some time a burden to his brothers. When he felt that these were becoming ill-disposed toward him, he borrowed a little money—quite possibly from the very same widow—and bought a number of palm-rib crates which he set out, filled with quantities of tomatoes, cucumbers, green beans, and windfall tangerines, in that very place. Then, in the early morning, alert and energetic, he started to receive his clients.

News of this important commercial enterprise of my uncle's soon spread to every part of the village, causing his brothers and the rest of the family to leap to the defense of the honor that was on the verge of being sullied within the confines of the as yet unfinished mosque, and hurried fatwas were issued from the depths of the aeries of the other families that supported our cause, proving beyond the shadow of a doubt that the use of a mosque for purposes of buying and selling—irrespective of whether it be incomplete and irrespective of whether any should undertake to clean it—constituted the purest profanity, and that it were better that the mosque be razed to the ground than left for some skirt-chaser to practice such shameful deeds in during the day (and no one, naturally, mentioned what he might get up to there during the night).

The logical conclusion was that the mosque would have to be finished, and other families deployed their forces to assist us in the task. However, with an upward gesture of the hand, one of our family's peerless heroes proclaimed his refusal of any such assistance, for the matter concerned us and us alone.

So the family sold a distant piece of land that was not bringing in a worthwhile rent (some of them using this as an occasion to ponder why God had blessed my grandfather's wealth and why this blessing had not trickled down to the rest of the family) and set to work again on the building.

The walls had risen a number of meters and the features of the mosque had taken shape almost to neck level when a building inspector swooped down upon the village.

Who was responsible for the building? My middle uncle on my father's side, the strong one who wasn't lame, stepped forward and said, as though preparing himself to receive an award, "I am the one responsible."

The government took this mighty uncle off with it, at the beginning of 1937, and left him to spend two months in prison, with hard labor, for erecting a public building without recourse to the authorities and without obtaining the necessary permit. The village put its hand over its mouth in disbelief, perhaps, or in amazement, or perturbation, or mockery, or embarrassment. What is sure is that the work stopped and the dogs, wasps, and putrid waters started to collect again, whilst the activities of the bats reached a level exceeding any achieved by the aforementioned.

My older brother was a man, in the full sense of the word. He was made of a different clay from my grandfather or any of my paternal uncles. He obtained his elementary school diploma, and then his maternal aunts (who are not *my* maternal aunts) managed to find him a job with the district council in Asyut. He took up residence in a place far away from us, and his home became a haven for most of the people of the village: anyone who had a court case in Asyut, was wanted by the army, desired to bribe the irrigation inspector, or felt like wasting a few pounds of the money from the cotton harvest would go to see my brother and there take up quarters until his mission was completed.

My brother became famous. More famous than Abd al-Alim the mayor and Ahmad Khamis the story-singer.

My brother was familiar with the progress of events concerning the building of the mosque, and he had also caught wind of discussions taking place at the district council concerning the need to construct schools in the village to educate (it goes without saying) the People.

My brother was not stupid. He came to the village and went over the matter with his siblings, explaining to them that the village was less in need of a mosque than of a school.

The village had thirteen mosques and numerous smaller places of worship, whereas its only school was part of an old mosque and was run, in return for grain and bread (both village-style and regular), by Sheikh Abd al-Waddud, who was, regrettably, a member of a hostile family. Not to mention that education was second only to worship in God's eyes and that the business would bring them great profit. The school would be in their part of the village and it would have teachers, principals, and inspectors, plus a respectable monthly rent . . . . "So," said he, "give me your authorization to proceed!"

My brother received their authorization. He sold some land, obtained a building license, roofed the school, and expanded it to the left by buying an adjacent piece of land. Then he put up a second story and divided the floors into classrooms. Rubbing his hands in satisfaction, he departed, casting a backward look at the building. He was on his way to the train station to finalize the matter in Asyut when he was confronted by the sight of a number of Bedouin putting up tents on the other side of the road and hammering in pegs.

"What's going on, boys?" he asked.

"We're Survey Department workers," they replied, "and we're laying out the site for the new school."

Then one of those with the massive hats came over to him and said, after greetings, "We're in a hurry, see. We have to hand it over to the contractor the day after tomorrow so that he can get it built before winter."

My brother dropped dead and was buried in April 1950.

My name is So-and-so. I graduated two years ago from the Faculty of Humanities. I do a little light work—such as giving private lessons—while waiting to be appointed to a teaching position.

During a bus tour of Europe I became acquainted with some French people and I invited them to visit our village, an invitation that they are now honoring.

Among the group is a woman called Marina. She is beautiful, talkative, and endowed with certain distinguishing personal traits, such as the ability to get wildly enthusiastic wherever and however she might find herself.

Marina spotted the building. She took it all in with her green eyes. Then she shouted out something that meant that it was wonderful and that she was ready to put everything she possessed into setting up a rest house for tourists coming and going on the Upper Egypt highway to and from Luxor and Aswan.

Her ideas were modern and clear. The building was wonderful and the road, which ran the length of Upper Egypt, was only a stone's throw away. Marina wanted to bring her sister, who dances in cheap entertainment establishments, to add some warmth to the place. It was all logical and satisfactory.

The Battle of the Camel

Siesta time dragged the people and the animals off the streets and the dykes and cast them down on the mud benches and inside the byres and the houses. Sheikh Abd al-Aziz Khalil (ninety-two years of age) described the weather that day as 'hell' and his sole remaining wife (bedridden) responded that "God alone is kind."

Hajj Nadir locked up his shop and hurried to the courtyard of the mosque where he flopped, I mean dropped, down panting and without even tossing a greeting to the lifeless bodies of Muhammad Abd al-Majid, Abd al-Nazir Ibrahim, Abu Zayd, and Ga'ud. Even the flies, dogs, and gypsies gave up and slunk away.

The whole village lay becalmed, though not asleep, beneath the walls, next to the water butts, in the shade, and not a breath of air was to be found that might push aside the mountain that sat on people's chests.

Suddenly a man passed along the village paths. He threw himself at the doors, beating on them hard and crying, "Your friend has arrived!" And the doors and windows opened.

Those in the open areas—of the mosque, at the market— were the first to move, though not the first to hear the news.

Initially it was just a spasm that shook them, but then they pulled themselves together, their bodies leaped into life, and they burst out onto the highways, followed by the rest of the folk. Their friend had arrived! Their objective was a low house with an iron-grilled window in its upper story and a door reinforced with iron bars (taken from those the village had obtained when it participated in the sacking and demolition of the police station of the nearby town during the 1919 revolution).

Within seconds, the folk had surrounded the house. Not a soul remained behind doors. All were present, gathered in that humid, low-lying place, their faces encircling the house, their voices reverberating in the air, the heat searing their skins, and they cried, "Open the door, Camel!"

But the Camel didn't open the door, or the window, leaving the undulating mass to surge this way and that.

"Come out, Camel!"

But the Camel didn't come out, so the strong ones hammered on the door with insistent blows, though the door was a block of iron.

"Open up, Camel!"

And the brickbats rained down on the door and the window, and the rough, repellent screaming of the women battered the ears, and the door remained closed, and the window remained closed.

"Let's knock the house down over his head!"

Huge rocks from the cemetery and the bottom of the hollow flew, shaking the walls and the door. The whole area was transformed into a thick cloud of dust, and one favored man discovered a sawn-off palm trunk, which the crowd lifted with a sudden, effortless, movement and used to ram the door, the dust cascading from the walls and the doorframe in the intervals between each blow.

The door started to give way.

Then the window opened. The Camel opened it himself and his terrified white face appeared between the bars, but when he was pelted with rocks and brickbats he closed it again.

"Come on out, Camel!"

The Camel opened the window a second time and extended a hand holding a white cloth and suddenly all eyes were fixed on the window. The white flag sucked up the yelling and the screaming and the commotion, and the Camel's voice screamed in entreaty, "I'll come out, on condition . . . . "

The silence held and the Camel went on ". . . that nobody lays a hand on the family."

The Mu'awda, Hadayda, and Firan clans were on the right, the Shinnawiya, 'Amaysha, and Awlad Jarban on the left, and in the center, directly under the eaves of the house, was everyone else.

Everyone moved backward and formed a semicircle around the door.

The door opened.

A small boy wearing a brightly patterned shirt and white trousers came out. He looked terrified and by the time he had moved a few centimeters beyond the door had no idea where he was going. He was followed by a thin little girl a year or two older wearing a dress with broad green stripes, her small hand waving in the air in an attempt to grasp hold of her brother.

The last sound disappeared and silence enveloped all.

A few seconds later the mother appeared, pale as saffron.

"Come out, Camel!"

The terrifying voices rose again and the two children had almost run back in terror into the house when a black billhook moved. A black billhook moved through the air and crashed at speed into the boy's head. Another fierce billhook split it open. The boy's head split open, his scalp fell to the ground, a third billhook flashed as it ripped through the little girl's neck and it—the neck—was thrown backward as another billhook was thrust upward with the white cloth on it.

A thick, disembodied hand reached out for the mother and pulled her forward a quarter meter and someone darted inside, dragged the Camel out by his neck, and threw him to the ground. Then the billhooks and mattocks descended, at one in their butchering, and chopped and chopped.

The Acacia Dog[1]

On my way home from the mill, after the bend in the sycomore-fig road, I met with a woman on the verge of the age of despair. Sensing that she desired intimate converse with me, I conveyed to her the feeling that I was not averse. The road emptied of all life. The trees, despite their enormous size, fled. Silence embraced us.

She asked about my father, and I indicated to her that he was dead, and that my mother had remarried. "A pity," she said, and I did not know at whom the pity was directed, my father or my mother. She was huge, profuse. She was not repulsive and I judged it better to ignore whatever particulars about her might be displeasing.

On the outskirts of town the woman turned off the road to the right, into the middle of the fields. I experienced a slight hesitation and feeling of fear by reason of the afreet that was known to appear in that place at high noon. The woman looked at me with her naive kohl-rimmed eyes that brimmed with all the ingredients of village seductiveness. I became drunk with desire and set off behind her. She stopped so that she might

---

1. An 'acacia dog' is a kind of small worm that grows on the branches of acacia trees in Upper Egypt.

walk beside me and asked after my brothers and I said, "The eldest we have not seen for nineteen years as the authorities are detaining him in one of their prisons, there to pass the period of imprisonment agreed upon with the superintendent of police." (Here the woman laughed at my wit.) "The second," I continued "is blind and ekes out a living pouring the chapters of the last thirtieth of the Qur'an over the openings of graves; the third is a teacher at an elementary school that appeared in the days of Taha Hussein's theory about education and water and air and how everyone was supposed to have access to them; the fourth is I" (who walk here beside you, envelop your body in my glances, and strain my faculties to extract something acceptable from your attractions). My sweat flowed and my shoes filled with dust as I bent over to tie my laces and continued, "and the fifth, the youngest of us, finished his schooling two years ago and is now performing his military service."

"And your sisters?"

"The eldest wed, then died giving birth. The second is at home and has not yet married."

At a tin shack sleeping beneath an acacia tree, the woman stopped, produced a key from the braids of her hair, and applied herself to opening the door. I leaned my back against the acacia. Within seconds, two acacia dogs had crept into my clothes. The worm-dogs horrified me. I removed my jallabiya, flung it on the ground in panic, and inspected my undergarments lest the worms had got that far. Several times the woman wetted the key with her spittle, laughing in delight at my agitation. The sun joined forces with my senses to stir my desire, and a lovely redness spread over her cheek. Her hair was long and smooth and clean.

"What put your brother in prison?' she asked.

"Drugs."

The woman said she was sorry and fell silent.

She asked me who had been the cause of my second brother's blindness. I told her that the enemies had cast a spell on him and he had fallen sick with smallpox when twenty years old, the disease inflaming his eyes. Once again, she said she was sorry and fell silent. Then she opened the door for me.

She sat down on an ancient mat. I removed my shoes and she herself took them and set them far from where we were sitting, for they smelled bad.

"And what do you do now?" she asked.

"Nothing."

She said she was sorry and asked of my younger brother's condition. I talked at length of his state, for today he is the best man in the whole village, even though he suffers from the problems we thrust upon him from time to time and does not often come, though he does write to us. She made me tea, then asked if I could smell the smell of a particular thing. The woman looked at my shoes and laughed, and her femininity became yet clearer. Her buttocks were fat and her body plump. Her arms were beautiful and her hands a wonder. She took off her clothes and smiled at me to encourage me. I removed my undershirt and looked at her, to start the matter, but she moved away from me coquettishly.

"Have you been to Cairo?" she asked.

"I have not," I replied.

"Have you seen what the girls of Cairo do to young men?" she inquired.

"I have not, but I have an idea of what happens," I said.

"Why did your father die?" she asked.

"I do not know," I replied. Then I corrected myself and told her that he had died in the fields, or so it was said.

"How?" she asked me, but I could not answer.

"Very well, why did your mother marry again?" she asked.

"Because she had to," I replied.

Her face blushed more deeply. She said she wished she could become acquainted with my younger brother who was in the army. I expressed my gratitude and promised her that, at the first opportunity, I would bring him to her boudoir here in the tin shack.

She said, "I shall feed you."

I did not refuse. She brought out a large metal can of pungent cured fish. I did not relish the thought of eating it and showed her my annoyance.

She said, "This rotten fish is the essence of the hearts and guts of most of the young men in the area." I laughed, but she . . . she was frowning.

The woman stood to take something from a high shelf and I realized that she was beautiful, very beautiful indeed. In no way was there any relation between this woman and the one who had come in with me from the outside, except in overall appearance. She was beautiful and that was all.

I stood and embraced her. She shrank back coyly and kissed me. She started asking me questions again, so I closed her mouth with my hand as I held her, a body smooth and burning, afire, a woman at her peak.

"Don't speak," I said, "for all my world is hungry dogs that crawl on acacia trees burned by the sun."

I pressed down on her with all the cruelty and tenderness of pleasure but she started to squirm from my grip. I pressed harder.

"Your mother married the man she had known before your father. Your father was burned while stealing from an orphan's field. Your sister died giving birth to an ape. Your older brother . . . ."

I pressed harder still. Her hair vanished, her voice changed, and she grew a mustache. I struck her. I struck her to close that twisted mouth. I struck her hard and with all the force of the palm of my hand. The woman recoiled in alarm. She recoiled in alarm and stood upright—black, covered in coarse hair all the way to her hooves, her hooves. "God is great!" I cried, and she spat on my face. "God is great!" I cried again, and the sparks flew from her eyes. "God is great and I seek refuge with Him from lapidated Satan!" I cried, and she said, "You are your father and your mother, your sister and your brother." My guts shrank, my eyes rolled, and I felt the terrors of the next world envelop me under the high noon of this. My body flattened out on the ground and I could find no backbone to hold me erect and support my height. The woman pulled me along by my feet and flung me outside the shack. Tired and naked, I crawled up the trunk of the acacia tree.

It was hot and I was utterly naked. I tried to determine the location of the shack beneath the tree. The twists and furrows of the branches hid the ground and everything on it. I crawled, sad and lost, around and among the branches, thorns, and gum-mountains until I was quite exhausted. A summer breeze tugged at me and I dropped onto shining white cloth passing beneath the tree. The creature became aware of my presence. Agitated, it picked me off its shoulder. Then it threw me to the ground and squashed me with its slipper, leaving me to writhe, and went its way.

Assassination

They were leaving the mosque of the Sons of Abdillah right after the evening prayer. Each looked hesitantly at the other, seeking to rid himself of whomever or whatever it was that troubled him, and they made their way quietly to the meeting ground outside the house of Hajj K.

On the wooden bench (made by Jabra the carpenter, who had yet to receive the money he was owed for it) sat D and S, while on a low bench of mud brick built into the wall sat other letters of the alphabet. Two more consecutive letters were standing because they were too young to be allowed to sit.

A lad came in with a clay brazier and set it down close to the mud bench. Being nervous and unskilled, he dropped some burning coals on the ground. One of the men pushed a fallen slipper out of the way, then calmly extended his fingers to the coals, picked them up, and returned them to the brazier.

D spoke and S interrupted him, and they threw the matter open for discussion by the others, who sipped their tea, chewed their tobacco, and spat on the ground. One of them expressed, once again, his admiration for the new imam of the mosque. Another objected, contrasting the different qualities of the new imam and the old. Another found fault with the behavior of one of the schoolteachers, who played cards in Farghali Mursi's café, and someone else announced his belief that Sheikh F would be let out of prison next Revolution Day. One went to great lengths over the description of the cow that had fallen into the watering-trough and which, in order to save, they had had to slaughter, and another, a young man, bent over the brazier and turned the coals, releasing a cloud of smoke. Someone asked someone else to lend him two keelas of corn, from which the second excused himself, swearing that his granary bin was devoid of even a single grain, which everyone knew to be a lie.

The conversation having died out, Hajj K broached the critical topic and threw it vehemently among them. When they proved themselves slow to pick up on the topic thus thrown, Hajj K, with yet greater passion, leaped up and threatened one of them who'd dozed off with a cuff to the back of the neck, cursing him and telling him contemptuously that he would turn out just like his maternal uncle, who slept at funerals. At this point one of the letters that hadn't spoken rose and tried to calm him down, pulling him toward the bench, but Hajj K refused to sit. He remained standing, furious and silent. Then he chose three—one of the ones sitting down, one of the ones standing up, and one who had yet to appear—and ordered them to take care of it.

Little discernment would have been needed for us to elucidate the outcome of the meeting, which was that these three men had been chosen to kill Mrs. H.

The next morning, the first two made their way to the third, the one who had failed to turn up, to inform him of the decision and agree on a time to undertake of the killing of Mrs. H.

The third wasn't at home, so they made their way to the market and thence to the North Side, where they ate some bread and ta'miya from a woman's stall and then seated themselves in a store, where they puffed molasses-soaked tobacco. A customer was telling the story of the difficulties he'd encountered trying to sell his taro in Cairo's Rod al-Faraj market. The speaker soon arrived at the meat of his story, which was that he'd met there a woman trader who resembled a certain well-known dancer and that this woman had fallen passionately in love with him, even though the speaker had tended toward sternness in his dealings with her, for he had felt it important to make it clear to her that he was in no way similar to the people of Cairo. The owner of the store turned the dial on the radio to a station playing love songs.

Having tuned the radio, the owner turned to the counter and settled down to listen to the blend of sounds, while the speaker pressed on deeper and deeper into the labyrinth of his tale. His listeners sat still as mice. He had reached the point where the lovelorn woman invited the object of her affections to visit her at home, and the listeners' features had poked themselves above the horizon, focused, and begun sweeping the airwaves, eager to seize on any signal that might issue from the speaker's mouth so that they might decode it, instantaneously, into whispers, eyes, thighs, hard breathing, a mouth masticating gum, desire, and a luxurious bed with a radio, a glass of tea, and a roast chicken next to it . . . when an old woman burst in on them and approached the owner of the store to buy a piaster's worth of sugar, a piaster's worth of rice, a match, and a sixty-para piece of soap. By the time she had left, the day's installment of the radio soap opera had begun to pour itself into the listeners' skulls and they had burst into such vociferous commentary that the speaker and his tale fell silent and the lovelorn market woman had to stand waiting in a corner. The old woman made for the door with her purchases, but stopped on the threshold and peered into her hand with a rheumy eye to make sure that the coin there was a one-piaster and not a ten-piaster piece. The tea flowed down the sides of the kettle and over the stove, causing green and violet flames to leap up, only to die down once more. The storyteller and object of desire was poised to continue the tale that had been interrupted. The two men charged with the killing of Mrs. H sat in silence.

At that moment, in the distance, the third man, the one chosen to complete the group and for whom they had been looking, passed by. The second stood up and called out at the top of his voice. The third took notice and turned aside, making his way toward them. On the radio, the Seductress, loading her voice with every ounce of seductiveness she could muster, had just begun to pour it into the ear of the Leader of the Gang and onto the counter, across the floor, and over the listeners' heads, and the owner of the store had just held his round watch to his ear to make sure it was running in preparation for the sunset prayer, when they were rudely interrupted by the second man's shout. Equanimity returned to the store when the two went out to meet their teammate on the road.

Without preamble, one of the two rammed the whole story into the ear of the third, who made a little pile of dust on the ground with his foot as he listened. Then he brought out his tobacco tin, tossed some into his mouth, and began to chew. He asked them if the job had to be done that night. Yes, Hajj K had said that night. The third shook his head from side to side in refusal. The first intervened to impress upon him the importance the family attached to Mrs. H's being killed that night, but the third said he had to go that night to the Circle of Remembrance at the tomb of Sidi al-Sheikh Salama.

"After the dhikr, then," said the second. There was a period of silence. The third said that in any case he'd try if it finished early but suggested that they put the whole thing off till the next day. Another period of silence. When he saw that the two weren't going to give him the delay he wanted, he said, "Very well," and went his way.

On the radio, the eventful episode came to an end and the announcer declared that the next installment would air the following day. Eyes began to withdraw from distant horizons and gather once again on the face of the storyteller, asking the market woman's lover to go on, and a single rusty spoon stirred the contents of each glass of tea set out on the counter.

Bughayli Bridge

From the beginning—and even long before the beginning—we have had to put our faith in the fact that fish dwell in water, bats in ruins, teachers in schools, peace of mind in death, foxes in fields, monks in monasteries, falsehood in books, seeds in cracks, poison in menstrual blood, and wisdom in the aftermath of events; and the best of you, good gentlemen, is the one who is spared either the wisdom or the events.

Talk of wisdom brings to mind our friend the police officer, who, a few days prior to his being awarded the Badge of Courage, had been stabbed by a thief he wasn't chasing and arrested a murderer he wasn't looking for. Most villages would commit their crime and then present our friend with tea, the corpse, the murderer, and some wisdom, or, on a few occasions, with the corpse, the wisdom, and the murderer, hiding the tea. Once a certain village put on a feast for this police officer friend of ours, thus winning him over before presenting him with the crime and the murderer, but hiding from him the corpse, the wisdom, three of his men, and the tea, and in the end he was obliged to shoot a dog that had impeded the investigation—indeed, the investigations—with

24

its incessant howling. Indeed, all matters trickle and flow, twist and intersect, spread themselves out and seldom come together, so that it was a terrible day when our village broke all the unwritten rules by killing one of its men—killing him in his bed and smashing his skull—and presenting him in the morning to the stubborn police officer sans wisdom, murderer, or tea, and sans even—so devoted were they to wisdom—the murder weapon, and we spent so many days dodging and evading the officer and placing before him and in his papers skillful answers to exasperated questions, that eventually he was obliged to force his way into the houses, open the closets, break into the byres, scratch around in the granaries, turn upside down the pots and pans, and sift the dust of the bakery, as well as interrogate the women, the chickens, the dogs, the gossips, and the little children; all of which left him only more exasperated and led him, on the seventh day, to swear that he would cut off his right arm if he failed to find the murderer. On the night of the ninth day, a message was slipped to him by the Snooper of the Northern Sector, at which point our friend the officer discovered that the perpetrator had thrown the murder weapon into the Dayrutiya canal—under Bughayli Bridge, to be precise.

Had you been in the officer's place, you would have paid no more attention to this message than you would have to the business of his cutting off his right arm (even though the description of the murder weapon in the riddling message answered precisely to that deduced by the medical examiner), and that would be because Bughayli Bridge, dear believers, is haunted—by three devils, a black slave girl, and an ape, all of whom have dwelt since time immemorial beneath its stanchions. Trustworthy persons have reported seeing with their own eyes the devils, the slave girl, and the ape emerge from under the bridge and play hopscotch on its surface, and it is said that the devils (and here we invoke the name of God the Merciful, the Compassionate) play other, more scandalous, games with the ape, or the slave girl, and that, as night falls, the sycamore-fig trees rise massive, black, towering, and gigantic to interpose themselves between this crew and any who dare penetrate its playground.

The police officer, however—out of solicitude, perhaps, for the arm that he'd sworn to amputate—gave no weight to this honest advice, presented with exquisite politeness by the village sheikh, and ordered a diver from the Department of Bridges to be brought, asserting that no call had been made for such a diver for, oooh, twenty-three years. One morning, therefore, we were presented with the sight of the obdurate officer assaulting Bughayli Bridge with a convoy whose primary components were two cars, a boat, policemen, and a diver equipped with a helmet, a leather suit, and various tools and kit, while he—alertly, keenly—stood nearby and ordered his men to spread out along the banks.

On days when we feel disposed to be more than normally wise, we prefer to be benign, ingratiating, and kindly, in that it is given to us to observe the police while they are preoccupied with our own affairs. The task was clear from the beginning—one dive, or two, to allow the diver to discover the cleaver with which our village had ripped into the dead man's skull and when we assembled (and even before we assembled) around the bridge, we were completely submissive to the instructions that had been given: not to approach the bridge (so we didn't approach the bridge), not to talk (so we didn't talk), and not to let out any screams (and fifty hands clapped themselves over the mouths of any who did so). The diver remained on the bank, taking clothes off and putting clothes on, and then

taking them off again. Then he put on the leather suit, followed
by the helmet. Three policemen surrounded the diver in order
to adjust the helmet on his head, and we felt a keen happiness.
I, personally, wished I might be granted the opportunity to
kill a man every night so that the next morning I could enjoy
the sight of the diver putting on his helmet. Then the diver
moved toward the water with the same slow pride displayed
by Sheikh Muhammad Mabruk when he slew his wife's sister
in the marketplace.

The diver disappeared into the waters next to the boat and a
shudder and a dampness swept over us. The diver didn't come
up, and we almost choked. Then he surfaced, but before we
could breathe a sigh of relief he had disappeared once more.
This time he was gone so long we got used to his not being
there, but then he came up and raised his arm in a dismissive
gesture, at which the officer yelled at him to be a man and
get on with it, for what he was looking for wasn't a knife, or
a sickle, or a shaving razor; it was a cleaver—"a cleaver, man,
not less than thirty centimeters in length and weighing four
pounds!" A woman started screaming again and we were all
embarrassed. Holding onto the side of the boat, the diver
rested his back against one of the piers of the bridge, raised
the front plate of the helmet from his face, and announced
that he couldn't reach the bottom—behavior that we dimly
recognized as a translation of a message sent us by the crew of
devils, for, though the officer believed that he was capable of
anything, on land or beneath the bridge, if he had listened to
us he would have withdrawn his men, his boat, and his diver,
untethered his two cars, and gone away, for, you see, the canal
might remain full to the brim, so that you might almost think
that it was the Great River itself, and then dry up and turn to
patches of mud where children and gatherers of shellfish and

shells could play, but never the area around Bughayli Bridge, which would remain forever full of water—deep, profound, wild, and unconnected to the rest of the canal, shrouded in an awesome and terrifying eternal darkness of branches and tangled plants that fiercely embraced the bridge's piers. But who other than us would understand such things? So the officer went back to shouting at the diver, the helmet had to like it or lump it, and a sensation of pleasure rippled through our assembled throng.

The waters boiled, and we continued to watch closely the spot where the diver had disappeared. Then the tangled weeds spread themselves out and we watched even more intently. Every time the weeds moved under the bridge we held our breaths, and a man who had won a bet by crossing the bridge in the middle of the night two times said, "Dear God, let the Hooded One show himself!" "And what might the Hooded One be, Sheikh Isma'il?" "The Hooded One is the serpent that has the jewel in its breast that lights up when it senses danger," said Sheikh Isma'il, and he took off to one side three youths of limited experience and tried to explain to their straitened minds everything he knew about the Hooded One. A mother of children whispered that the diver would, beyond doubt, lose the capacity to reproduce, but a girl, clearly recently married, recounted her feelings the night she had rolled over seven times on top of the bridge after the breaking of the spell that had made her bridegroom impotent. Then a garrulous grocer yawned and cursed the government, and when nobody responded by asking him why he was cursing the government, cursed the people, and when everyone's eyes remained fixed on the water following the slight ripples caused by the diver's movements, cursed the ones standing next to him, and when none of them bothered to pay his insults any attention either, hit the man standing in front of him on the back of the neck, which gave rise to a some minor bickering combined with a quarter-quarrel, which was nipped in the bud by a harsh unpleasant man with a few cutting words. And all the while our eyes were fixed on the eddies in the water, waiting to enjoy the sight of the cleaver with which we had smashed the skull of our friend in his bed. And the weeds on the piers spread and moved, providing evidence of unseen upheavals taking place at the roots of the world.

The silence continued to build and groups to form around the bridge, along the sides of the canal, and by the roots of the sycomore figs, the officer resolute and stern as a lion, smoking cigarettes, the diver unseen in the sunken world searching for the murder weapon. Then a dog broke through the ring of onlookers and into the empty area, looking at the officer so hard that we were sure he was about to say something. He, however, (the dog, that is) made for the railing of the bridge, scratched his back, and raised his right hind leg. At this, the crowd's tendency to bicker grew worse and someone suggested to someone else that it would be a good idea to slip over to the wheat field on the east bank where one could see better and, had not the diver surfaced at that moment, the officer would have yelled at them. Everyone craned their necks and the policemen lost no time in hurrying over to assist him in pulling out a metal tire rim. The crowds writhed and returned to their silence, and the diver to his diving. The sun had managed to climb higher and was bathing the tops of the sycomore figs with light, and a poor man came up to the officer in embarrassment and dread and asked him to instruct his men to take care not to trample the wheat, which was sparse and thin and covered the eastern bank, descending in rows till it almost touched the waters of the canal; and indeed, the officer signaled to his men to watch where they put their feet and the poor man set off happily to cross the bridge toward the wheat, but the officer shouted at him and told him to go back.

It now became obvious that the diver was laboring to pull something out. Everybody rushed forward and broke through the cordon, but they were seized and stopped. Then he appeared, clinging to the side of the boat. He carefully pulled out a cloth bag the color of mud with a splash of bright red on it and threw it into the bottom of the boat. The crowd heaved, but the officer shouted and his men rushed over to them as our eyes strained to make out what was in the bag. Some idiot yelled, "God damn! That's Sam'an's daughter's bag!" One of the onlookers closed the idiot's mouth with both hands.

We broke ranks. The bag stayed in the bottom of the boat. One of the policemen lowered a stick with a hook on it and used it to raise the bag from the boat and throw it onto the bridge. The officer approached it, prodded it with the tip of his shoe, and ordered one of his men to open it. It contained a piece of green fabric as from a woman's dress, a wooden key, and locks of hair. The officer looked hard at the contents, tapping his thigh with his swagger stick. The policemen worked together to push the people back to their original position so most of us resorted to climbing the sycamore-fig trees, but before things could settle down again, the diver had tossed a small skeleton into the boat. This was carefully raised to the bridge, a woman shrieking "Poor child!" and an old man announcing, as the bones were set out next to the bag, that they belonged to Sabir, the son of Sheikh Mas'ud. The sound of a woman sobbing quietly among the rows hung in people's ears and another woman reported, by way of correction, that they were the bones of the son of Sa'd the cripple, at which the old man told her, by way of further correction, that Sa'd's son had been burned to death, not cut down. The grocer then shouted that the skeleton belonged to the son of Rizq and started itemizing his evidence. He was unable to complete his exposition, however, because the diver had come back and thrown down a skull whose identification required no guesswork: among its front teeth shone a celebrated flash of gold; it was—oh my God!—the head of Salman the Gypsy. A young man began to wail, but two of his companions held him back, and the officer yelled that he had come here to look for the cleaver only, and everyone waited for him to continue. A woman prone to having children without benefit of husband laughed and shouted out in a serious voice, "And who's stopping you from pulling out the cleaver?" infuriating the officer, who ordered everyone to move farther away, but the crowds grew thicker—in the sycamore-fig trees, on the mud walls and the tombstones, and amid the wheat.

If, at that moment, the officer had called a halt and announced that he had failed to find what he was looking for, no one would have blamed him, but the bearer of the Badge of Courage determined to carry on. His men started working together to release a large thighbone entangled in the weeds, the thighbone of a camel. Certain individuals with a knowledge of thighbones laughed, and no sooner had the thighbone reached the top of the bridge than an old-timer announced that it was—he swore by his beard—the thighbone of the late Sheikh Hajj Hasan. Someone else contradicted him, invoking the name of the sainted Bibawi, and discussion groups formed among the knots of onlookers, with everyone trying to convince everyone else of his point of view. At this point, the diver threw down a collarbone with shreds of cloth still attached to it, and the whispers proceeded in a confused babble from which it might be deduced that the collarbone belonged (there could be no doubt about it) either to Hannuna, or Safyura, or Furayha, or the wife of Aziz Effendi. It also became obvious that the officer was still awaiting the discovery of the cleaver and the policemen began widening the laying-out area. Now—God protect us!—here were welded vertebrae from a spinal cord attached to an arm (Abbas al-Qadi, or Jabir al-Hajib), the lower half of a tall slim skeleton wearing dotted drawers (Sa'd al-Bannuta), and part of a rib cage to which were stuck the remains of a striped vest retaining a watch chain (Hamdan al-Gaffas).

Each new extraction, as it moved from the water to the bridge, drew after it the eyes of the people, the writhings of the crowd, the first stirrings of chaos, the screams of those most closely involved, and the exclamations—"I seek refuge with God!" "Have mercy upon us, O Lord!" "O Protector!" "Woe is us!"—of the naive, while the officer gave orders and bustled and smoked and, on the wide laying-out area on top of the bridge, set out the finds, which consisted of two skeletons, one small and one large, their arms around one another (Hajj Gamhawi and son), a foot still in its slipper, a skull tied to a rope, a rock with shoulder bones gripping it, an arm still holding a spike-fiddle, and a rib cage run through by a metal skewer. Everyone denied and explained and exchanged suppositions and dread and formed clumps and drew back and jumped from tree to tree and trampled the wheat and clapped hands over mouths. The sun, which had crept to the middle of the sky and was nailed above their heads, poured sweat and terror down upon them, as hands took turns to receive from the diver the mortal remains and lay them out.

At this point, a note of caution is called for. It no longer concerned us whether we loved or hated the police officer or cared about the tombstones smashed beneath the weight of the people or whether we protected the stalks of wheat belonging to the man who was screaming "Woe is us!" with a thousand others screaming of woe alongside him. The sycomore-fig branches bent and deposited people in the canal so the diver was no longer alone as he toiled to bring up what had lain decently hidden beneath the bridge. Now anyone who had any experience of jumping and swimming and diving joined him and every minute that passed drew with it people from the villages and skeletons from the bottom of the canal, screams from people's throats and suggestions from those with information. A woman went up to the officer and asked him to tell them to look for her daughter and her sister's husband. An elderly man came and requested that they search for his five children. People leaped from the land into the water and the ordinary people got mixed up with the police, the wheat fields with the tombstones. A policeman assaulted a woman who was cursing him and a young man stabbed a man beneath the armpit for no obvious reason. A man dragged a woman along by her leg in an attempt to throw her into the water and a youth fondled a girl from behind and she screamed. Ta'miya vendors, tea makers, and preparers of molasses-soaked tobacco for water pipes appeared.

The officer tried to gather his men so that they could protect the laying-out area, but no one could hear him. The diver pulled out two more skeletons, but they fell off the edge of the bridge and back into the water. The canal was chaos—confused, muddy, surging chaos—and the diver's helmet, detached, twinkled far from the boat. Feet trampled the skeletons, the skulls, and all the other things that had been pulled out. The officer extracted himself from the throng of people and retreated. He climbed onto a car and tried yelling, then pulled out his revolver and fired into the air, but the canal continued to seethe with people. One of God's holy fools approached and offered the officer a tin mug of water. The man stretched out his hand for the mug and raised it to his lips but didn't drink. In fact, he started firing once more into the air. A young girl came to him leading an aging blind man. The girl screamed at the officer through her sobs, pleading with him to look for her father and her mother (the officer kept firing into the air), for her father and her mother and her older sister (the mug was still in his hand and had not got close to his lips), for her mother and her father and her brother's children. The feet turned and retreated in a savage reversal. The aging blind man was separated from the girl, his arms stretched upward into the air, and he collided with the people pushing forward and backward. He howled. The officer yelled, "If you don't stop where you are, I'll shoot to kill." The angle bar of the bridge, and its right side, were dislodged. People fell into the water. The water of the canal filled with wheat stalks, turmoil, sycamore-fig branches, divers, peasant caps, arms, legs, timbers from the boat, and weeds from the bottom of the bridge. The spume scattered by the raging waves took on a bloody color, like that of wisdom.

Operation Kidnap Amira

We pulled up the green corn stalks, lopped off their tops, and made beautiful rifles out of them with butts of mud that we covered with red brick dust. A thrill of apprehension swept over us as we left the fields behind and infiltrated the village with our mud rifles for the first time, to participate in the party that the North Side was putting on to celebrate the acquittal of Hafiz Effendi in the case of the abduction, strangling, and throwing into the market well of a child from the Batran clan. That day we obtained a plentiful supply of the cigarettes handed out at the party and spent a quiet time smoking among the roots of the trees of Hajj Mitwalli's garden, where we judiciously reviewed certain matters.

On the second occasion, we stood, weapons draped in mourning weeds, after Abd al-Alim, the mayor, was murdered. He had been leaving his mansion when a blast from a roaring ten-shot two-piaster cartridge blew his guts out. The deputy mayor caught sight of us in the middle of the melee, beat us with his stick, and cursed our parents. A number of us received wounds, in the forms of bruises. Muhammad Tawfig and Awf cried, and four rifles were broken to pieces. That evening we met in the garden and bought cigarettes with the proceeds from our looting of Ibrahim Bukhayt's early tomatoes. We spent a while repairing the splits in the rifles and putting ourselves to rights, and by the time the cigarettes had run out we had decided to assassinate the deputy mayor, Hajj Ghalib. However, as we discussed the matter further it became apparent that it was beyond our powers to devise a coherent plan for breaking into Hajj Ghalib's house, which cowered behind a wall, a garden, and twenty dogs, so we decided to kill the village headman instead. Three of us objected on the grounds that Sheikh al-Shinnawi was a relation so we decided to kill the head constable, but it turned out that he was too busy changing the evidence that he'd given before the court against the murderer of Fanus, and night overtook us before we could arrive at a final decision.

We went back to the village and as we sat beneath the incandescent lamp trying to repair our rifles, we reminisced about our happy memories of Mahmud, the son of our paternal aunt Dawlat, he of the burning intelligence and amazing energy who'd been savaged by a rabid bitch and died. We felt sad for a while, but then Sayyid Abu Mahmud stood up and did an imitation of one of our fathers telling his son off for wandering into the middle of the corn fields, where loose types and criminals on the run might kidnap him and demand ransom. This set off a small battle and we made sides and started beating up on one another. Master, the sheikh who taught us our letters, passed by and looked at us through a half-open eye (he's not completely blind), so we were obliged to freeze suddenly and pretend to be dignified. Then Madani asked us to make a lightning raid on the boys of the North Side, and Madani's team broke into uproar and started making shooting noises with their mouths. Abd al-Karim (who later drowned in the Marj canal) proposed that we pull the lamp down, so one of us started shaking the wooden post, making the lamp swing from side to side, but a man from the Sha'ayba clan chased us away, cursing our mothers.

Later we regrouped under the lamp and caught our breath. The air was full of dust, the crickets were creaking, and the silence was hell. A woman passed by, walking slowly. She was carrying a basket of flour, so two of us ran after her and stuck a rifle barrel between her feet. The woman tripped and tumbled down and the flour went everywhere and filled the street. We disappeared into the darkness of the alleyways and entrances to the houses and the woman's sobs rent the universe. (When the wretched woman went to my father and complained, he swore to her that I hadn't left the house and had been sleeping since sunset in the upstairs room.) We kept out of sight until the woman had left with whatever flour she could salvage from the ground, then we sat down again under the lamp.

"Let's kidnap Amira daughter of Abd!"

"No, let's beat up your uncle Abd al-Tawwab!"

"Let's steal Hajja Furayha's ewe!"

"Let's beat up Hajj Zahir!"

"Let's slip Abd al-Rahim al-Shamandi some datura!"

"Let's kill Sheikh Sayyid Mabruk!"

"Let's kidnap Amira daughter of Abd!"

"Let's get a hoopoe's head and roast it and put it in her bed!"

"No, let's cast a spell on her!"

"Let's go see the ghawazees dancing!"

"We don't have any money."

"Let's steal Hajj Muhammad Abu Hasanayn's sugarcane!"

"Let's kidnap Amira daughter of Abd!"

"Let's pull her clothes up while she's walking!"

"Let's beat her father up in his store!"

"Let's steal Juljula's donkey!"
"Let's pull up Abd al-Aziz Abu Khalil's taro!"
"Let's put dirt in the stew at Malik's house!"
"Let's kidnap Amira daughter of Abd!"
"Enough! We'll kidnap Amira daughter of Abd!"
And we started to hop and dance, cock-a-hoop with joy.

At mid-afternoon the next day, we marched onto the streets, our rifles slung over our shoulders. Silent, swift, and purposeful we looked, and as fierce and hard as could be. We marched into al-Shinnawi Street and turned off onto al-Hayyid Lane. The lane was narrow and someone riding a donkey loaded with reeds was blocking it. We were forced to slow down, but eventually we got fed up and Ramzi Jad slipped under the load in a flash and got in front of the donkey. He pulled the donkey's rope out of its rider's hand, taking donkey and rider alike by surprise. The man yelled at the boy and the boy yelled at the man, telling him to move over so we could pass. The man looked angrily behind him and when he saw us—with our weapons—he laughed contemptuously. His behavior annoyed us, so one of us started hitting the donkey on its rump. The donkey was startled and bucked and the load collapsed onto the ground, trapping the rider beneath it. Someone else chased the donkey away. The man yelled at us from under the reeds, but three or four of us beat him on the head with the butts of our rifles. Then we jumped over him and set off in single file with our backs straight.

Someone asked the one behind him where we were going to kidnap Amira from—the house or the store. Someone else hit him on the back hard. We turned left, our eyes scanning the lanes for fear we'd catch sight of one of our fathers. We bumped into a beggar curled up at the foot of a wall. He was drooling, the saliva all over his chest. His eyes were dim and his head wobbled. We warned him to clear the path but the man started howling and asking God to grant us long lives, stretching his trembling arm toward us as he did so. Someone put out his hand and shook the beggar's to make fun of him and we laughed till we were giddy with joy and someone else filled his hands with dirt and poured it over the man's head. The man half rose, sobbing and calling for help, and one of us kicked him in the back. Two men came by, heading north, and drove us off, but they were laughing.

The Offering

We do not know exactly when it happened, but that it happened is certain. My father talked of it and my mother didn't deny it, and Yahya Haqqi, Yusuf Idris, Khalil Isa al-Ghar, Ali al-Juhayni, the Khwaja Bisada, the sainted Bibawi, and Abd al-Waddud the Nasal all went on about it. Abd al-Waddud the Nasal was the most emphatic in his insistence that it really happened, but it was Yusuf Idris who made the desperate efforts to pin down the period in which it occurred, and was even so bold as to state once that what happened had happened a long time ago, in the days of the plagues that engulfed Sodom and Gomorrah, to be precise.

Despite which we do not—in this present era of ours—possess any clear evidence that, if examined, would enable us to specify the time exactly. Were Sheikh Ali, the erudite scholar of the village, still alive, he would provide us with something to base ourselves on, for Sheikh Ali possessed a book with yellow pages and protected by spells which, it is said, the village had passed down secretly from hand to hand until it ended up in his keeping. It is also said that Sheikh Ali was burned to death while the book was in his possession. Indeed, it is said that the sheikh died as a result of his attempts to unravel those spells that concealed all the details we wanted to know. It is further said (and how many are the things that are said!) that the celebrated sheikh's spirit-sister took the village's spellbound book with her to her own village, behind the blue mountains, at the place where the sun sets.

I do not deny that what my folk differed over most was the time, the starting point, and the place of occurrence. Some believe that the South Side (where the mosque, tomb, and grave marker of Amir Sinan are situated) would be the most appropriate place for the beginning, others that the North Side (with the church, tomb, and grave marker of Amba Serapion) would be more so. A third party, mostly consisting of kinship groups foreign to the town, asserts that what happened started in the center of the town (where the houses of assignation, the brothels, the belly-dancing troupes, and the Ghawazee bands are concentrated).

No one, however, be he from the South, North, or Center, has ever tried—and this is a fact—to deny the happening itself.

1

The happening itself began at noon on a Friday (according to the account of Abd al-Waddud the Nasal).

Or on the morning of an Easter Saturday (according to the account of the sainted Bibawi).

A man from my village was sitting at the top end of his field intoning one of our celebrated songs of patience when his tongue became heavy and began to trip. The man became confused and panic-stricken. He had not become completely dumb, but the words that had been pouring from his larynx had lost their fluidity. They were ravaged in the depths of his throat and emerged as though crushed in a mill—mere letters, joined together by nothing but a stammering wail, stretched and taut.

The man stayed where he was, alone, trying to mould the sounds emerging from his throat. His lips, tongue, pharynx, the inner muscles of his cheek, and his palate struggled to link the letters, correct the words, order the particles, and beat the phonetic mob into submission, but in vain.

The man rushed to his house, his horror tucked under his arm—and not just under his arm, for he had also bitten off a great mouthful of it that was knocking about in his mouth and forcing yellow pallor, terror, and dread into his whole being.

My village rushed to stand by its son. Some appeared to practice magic and break the spell. Some arrived to bleed his brain and the place between his shoulders. Some came to take a piece of the afflicted man's clothing so they could burn it for their barren wives to step over seven times, after which these same wives would bathe on a moonlit night in water containing a frog with its throat slit. And some were there to explain the whole event away and pin it on the unbelief that had defiled the life of the sick man and caused him to abandon his religion and stop visiting the tombs of the saints.

But my village is fickle. It broke into commotion, it screamed, it offered solace, and it declared its opinion. Then it left things up to the one concerned, returning to its quarters convinced that what had happened had had to happen, for every now and then someone had to get bitten by a scorpion, or drown in the river, or have a wall collapse on him, or fall out of a palm tree, or meet our famous afreet Hawwash, who would terrify him into paralysis, or the Waterwheel Girl, who would corner him and scoop him up and carry him off with her to the well of a waterwheel or the cavity under a weir. Yes indeed, my village is fickle and it knows full well that it must, from time to time, play host to an event of this nature, when a certain predetermined percentage of its men has to be presented as an offering to fate—and thereafter let all not thus afflicted praise God.

In this way my village was able to satisfy itself as to the significance of the event before placing its arm beneath its head and going to sleep.

Things did not, however, stop with the dumbness of a single man. By the end of that same day a donkey trader had lost the power of speech without even having left his house, that his way might be blocked by the afreet Hawwash or the Waterwheel Girl.

Before the village could recover from its fear, an observant woman was struck dumb, and on the East Side a snake bit the tongue of the market supervisor, and the tongue of a statue maker was split in two. Five, six, sixty, a hundred, the whole village—even the pious preacher of its mosque, a man as white-hearted as milk and as kind as the prophet, a man as demure as a virgin, as gallant as a knight, and as brave as Ibn Abi Talib, this eloquent preacher opened his mouth as wide as it would go, there where he stood in the pulpit urging the believers to be patient, abandon sin, and cleave unto the ropes of the Creator—and his mouth stayed open. When the congregation noticed, they rushed to him and carried him away in an atmosphere of terror and affright that was filled with their mewings, croakings, and consternation.

Appeals had to be made to God and lips to be smacked in dismay.

But my village had been struck dumb. Its tongue had become paralyzed, the scales on it dissolving, and it could no longer form any of those mighty letters that make up speech. The village was struck dumb. Dismay afflicted its body and dizziness its head. Its eyes opened wide in terror. The disease had come upon it and it rushed right and left, importuning the houses of the saints and the tombs of the sheikhs and Allies of God, pounding mustard, fenugreek, sea ambrosia, lemongrass, and galangal and making out of them a concoction to drink on an empty stomach after rising, making a detour to the tombs where it sucked up the dirt, and then descending into the depths of the canals and water outlets to bathe or anoint its body with mud, pleading with the Lord at candle-lit altars and then praying every morning the two prostrations of the Prayer against Fright, cutting palm fronds and weaving them into crosses beneath which to sleep on moonlit nights and then pulling the crosses to pieces and rushing to the courtyard of the mosque to wail and call on the Only, the Victorious—all in an attempt to outmaneuver its terrible malady but ending up outmaneuvered by it. For it would return to itself only to find the dumb impossible still balled up in its mouth and itself still powerless to marshal letter beside letter, order word after word, and failing, at the end of the day, to form a sentence. Or if, on rare occasions, it succeeded in marshalling letter next to letter and ordering word after word, it would discover that the sentence it had arrived at was not the sentence it had sought, but a shredded, smashed, fragmented, truncated speech that dribbled from wide open mouths within which a tongue of cold, soft, flesh lay prostrate in a lake of spittle.

Toilsome were the efforts they expended to arrive at the secret of the calamity and to diagnose the disaster. They approached certain people of knowledge and miracles in the surrounding areas and slaughtered sheep and turkeys in their honor. They suffered the swallowing or chewing of amulets and were forced to jump over circular pits of fire fuming with incense, rats' tails, and insects' legs. They sought the help of the gypsies and Bedouin who passed their way, and the village filled with quacks and magicians, people with second sight and others who kept company with devils. And when their tribulation remained unchanged, delegations journeyed to Kordofan, Siwa, and Wadi al-Masakhit. Each returned with his own explanation and justification: a ruling from the oases said that someone in the village must, beyond any doubt, have sinned with his mother or father; according to another report, someone from the village must have practiced the Shameful Act on sacks of wheat, so that the blessed staff of life itself had become angry.

I should mention finally that among the attempts to undo the spell cast upon the village was one that required the slaughter of a red-headed orphan and the smearing of his blood on the buttocks of the men and the inner thighs of the women. When the village actually prepared this cure using a child they had abducted from a neighboring hamlet, and when the neighboring hamlet discovered that its red-headed orphan had gone missing, and after it came to their knowledge that he had been transformed into a potion to cure the village of dumbness, the furious people of the hamlet surrounded the village and entered it by force, slaughtering a number of its sons and menfolk, insulting eight of its women, and urinating on the faces of a hundred of its elders, with the result that my village desisted from testing further solutions.

2

Dismay continued to press down upon the breast of my village, silently, savagely, wildly. True, the fields dried up and poverty and yellowness afflicted them. True, the paintwork on the houses cracked and mud bricks fell from the sides of the door frames. True, the animals aborted and their udders went dry. And true, dust stained the people's faces, beards, and turbans. But none of that, none of it at all, was what mattered to my village. What mattered was its tongue.

My village was in no way whatsoever involved in manual labor. It was a trading village, all of whose elders and leading men were merchants—merchants in calves, buffaloes, chickens, bran and flour siftings, honey, grains, and vegetables. They depended above anything else on that jewel of a muscle, the tongue. With their tongues they paid compliments, argued, enticed, and invoked the Living, Eternal God and the holy books, and with their tongues they praised, lied, slandered, defended, and whiled away the evenings in agreeable converse. It was a flexible, mobile, tongue that remained constantly at play inside their mouths until that moment when it would pull out the appropriate sentence, whisper the loveliest, most radiant, and most delicate words, and spit out the harshest and most abominable utterances. It would sniff and savor, this ancient tongue, and roam and tour in the markets and at weddings, and then return to the houses with the most ample profits; a tongue sweet and responsive at whose singing every body in the area started to dance—fluent, super-exquisite, smooth, glad, a tongue that wriggled in the depths of wisdom, legend, and story. How many lands and cities did Abu Zayd, through the tongue of my village, invade, and conquer! Over how many walls and to the foot of how many battlements did Mercurial Ali, using the same means, leap, to disappear or to stand and fight! How far did Hasan the famous troubadour wander in search of his Na'ima, the tongue of my village unrolling before him plains and valleys that he might be carefree and sing and meet with his beloved! Even that ancient, terrifying tale, the tale of the man who murdered his brother, ripped his corpse to pieces, and scattered it throughout the region, became, on the tongue of my village, a warm and dreamy story telling of how the wife of the murdered man gathered his remains and brought them back to life.

There is no might and no power but in God. Behold our ancient tongue now retracted, shrunken, and benumbed, sleeping on the cast-off swaddling bands of speech as it lay tattered and collapsed on the floor of the throat! Behold the green songs of joy wither, the cheerful comments curdle, the laugh, once deep and broad, go flaccid, and naught but gloom and hissing remain!

3

My village remained in this state for a time—some say a month, some a year, some a hundred years—before it took a grip on itself, stiffened its resolve, dragged its exhausted body from the houses of the saints and the befrogged baths, and returned to its fields and beasts, its crops and palm trees, and all its other business. Hunger, nakedness, and the mockeries of the surrounding villages had worn it down. It had been rocked to its foundations but hastened to take charge once more of its affairs, convulsed as those might be. Arms, legs, and muscles set to work, turning ruined waterwheels, opening irrigation ditches, moving dirt, boring wells, and digging outlet channels. My village, speech-deprived, silent, and emaciated, moved toward its land, its trees, its vessels, its braziers, its ovens, and the tethering places of its animals. Loss of speech is a catastrophe, but hunger will make a man forswear his faith, and though speech be a necessity, the right of the gut takes precedence. At this point, my village started, slowly and in sorrow, to put its affairs in order again, for if the tongue had died, the other members—the eyes, arms, feet, reproductive member, heart, and brain—remained alive and in working order and it was the job of the tongue to allow its energy and powers to seep into the rest of the body's substance. Thus my village resorted to our first, primitive, ancient language, dusting it off and restoring it to pristine newness and returned to the sign and the art of the sign, that curious, ancient art, that solution held in reserve for any crisis the tongue may face.

The village began to develop the effectiveness of sign language. True, it might mew, croak, and make drawn out sounds, but it was through movements of the hands, the eyebrows, and the mouth, and noddings of the head, that it was able to forget, or pretend to forget. In any case, it moved. It moved away from the memory of the first days of its trial and that before its powers of speech had withered completely away, as soon, indeed, as it became clear that he who could produce a properly formed sentence was no better off than he who could produce only a mangled one. In any case, it moved. It moved to its beasts, to take them out into the open air, to its crops and trees, to help their growth and tend them, to its houses, to rebuild their collapsing walls, and to its mud-brick benches, to remove them entirely from before the doorways, for there was no longer any reason for people to keep company with one another of an evening. Soon mosques with no minarets appeared on the skyline, for the people had substituted for the exhortatory voice mere bangings on metal sheets or drums to call men to the performance of the mandated prayers. Next it was the turn of the eyes and ears to assume a new importance, and it became a duty to listen carefully for the lightest of light hisses, to be alert to the slightest of slight movements. They busied themselves with the art of the sign, improving it and inventing new gestures, not just for rapid communication when haste was imperative, but also for the telling of stories. My village became capable, even, of recounting the tales of wonder, such as those of the Man with the Flayed Leg, the She-ghoul, Clever Hasan, and Thimble and the Moon of All Moons. Indeed, it reached a point where the two arms could reproduce, in miniature, all the effects of the tongue and even tell jokes, puzzles, riddles, and funny stories, and there came a time when my village used to tell—yes, tell—stories that included anecdotes about a man who could speak, just as nowadays we might tell an anecdote about a man who was dumb.

4

The fields and the river banks revived despite the withering of the tongue, but the village's trade lay fallow. Certainly, you might do business once, for example, with a trader who couldn't speak, but you would not be able to deal on a permanent basis with all the speechless traders of the village. True, the traders attempted to compensate with their hands for what their tongues were incapable of making plain, but trade has another side, one that calls for whispers and shouts, persuasion and concession. My village might not have taken very long to return to its fields, but it was totally incapable of returning to the world of trade, for the fields, in the end, were under their owners' control, whereas in trade the villagers were only one party, and a party that found the greatest difficulty in convincing the other parties to do business with it, especially when those other parties were the rival villages that crowded the broad river valley and with which my village had clashed when it slaughtered the red-headed orphan.

Many are the reports that have come down to us on this matter. It is rumored, for example, that the traders' businesses failed and that the traders then melted into the mass of peasants and were assimilated among them, becoming landowners, renters, or day laborers. It was also claimed that the traders were transformed into simple middlemen, whose modest aspirations were limited to the villagers' internal dealings, and likewise, by way of further example, that the traders abandoned their village and infiltrated themselves into other distant villages far from one another, each of which was capable of supporting a single dumb trader. All of this meant that our village set sail for the shore, seeking for itself other affairs that were in harmony with any road it might take.

It is said that my village, having been deprived of its evening gatherings and convivial assemblies and finding difficulty in communicating its stories and scandals, its complaints and individual adventures, was compelled to invent other gatherings that did not employ the tongue, gatherings that had their own special means of providing pleasure. The tongue had withered away and its sound had been silenced, true enough; but the village took refuge in the palms of hands — the palms of its own hands. It was slow work at first and palm continued to strike palm only in order to announce certain small affairs — to call someone, or to denote approval or disapproval or refusal or anger. Then, quickly, the palms devised for themselves a special form of clapping that was comfortable and entertaining. A brand new art, the art of clapping, began to enter the blood and marrow of the village and take the place of songs, stories, evening discourse, curious anecdotes, and everything else for which recourse had been made to speech, letters, words, opinions, and argument. My village found itself realizing itself in clapping, in its variegation, until this came to constitute sufficient raw material for its entertainment, and nightly gatherings and parties were held that were based thereon. The village might seek the assistance of a singer from outside, but there can be no doubt that merriment, joy, and social cohesion had their source in those unerring, artistic, well-schooled palms. Indeed, with time, it became an easy thing to hold an evening party without a singer at all, the dancer gliding into the midst of a circle quivering to the gladdening beat of palms, a beat implanted deep in the body and heart—the beat of palms on palms, of palms on backs or on knees, on cheeks or on legs. Medleys and rhythms were born out of my village's genuine desire to enjoy itself and forget what was over and done with. There even came a time when the people of my village would invade the nocturnal gatherings and wedding parties of the other villages, despite all the constraints. And while it was possible that you might find in the other villages a gifted singer, dancer, or instrumentalist, you would certainly find that all the clappers were from mine.

Where trade failed to provide for my village, the art of clapping succeeded. A wedding would be put on in a settlement on the other side of the mountain, and the impresario would invite our people to perform. Art swept away, as it usually does, all the reservations and fears that, for a while, had constrained my village's movements, and the other villages, without exception, acknowledged the right of my village to participate in any wedding or social occasion. And it went beyond a mere matter of bands of clappers to encompass the training of the ghawazees and the selection and preparation of the most beautiful, supple, and fresh-faced of their daughters. The whole valley quivered at the magical, fetching, wordless beauty that swayed before it, freighted with everything that might arouse. The former traders, or their grandsons, or their grandsons' grandsons, found themselves at ease with this new market in whose efflorescence they were able to discover a living for themselves, and the village became crowded with bands—ghawazees, women solo dancers, players of the zummar, clappers, organizers, and impresarios—and the money flowed in, compensating them for what they had lost with the disappearance of their tongue. It no longer saddened the village that its mouth had been transformed into nothing more than an empty cavity seeking nourishment, or a thing with which they did no more than breathe. What had been absurd and shameful became, in this new dispensation, an advantage and a sign of distinction, and the mansions of the traders of the villages of the valley filled with men and women from my village who worked for them as guardians and nannies of their children. These would keep the secrets of the houses and preserve their privacy. They alone were the witnesses, but their mouths were sealed, incapable of revealing anything that might do the family harm, lower its prestige, or bring it shame.

5

The new businesses brought my village to the peak of its resurgence. The time when its sons and daughters worked as hired performers at weddings and soirées ended. Instead they began to negotiate their own contracts for the organization of festivities such as these and others recently invented. The village became intoxicated with its squares, which blossomed with joy, dancing, clapping, and fun. In no time, the weddings and good times swung out of the houses, squares, and streets and took to the fields. Some families grew famous for providing the most sumptuous food, others for providing the most splendid dancers, and yet others for hosting the costliest and most luxurious events. The village awoke to the value of its grapes and dried them and distilled them. It squeezed its sugarcane and fermented it. It dug long burrows beneath the houses and stored in these vaults beer and arak from Zahle. Certain particularly gifted individuals were able to create numerous recipes for the enhancement of sexual potency. Hashish and opium became widespread and were grown over wide swathes of village land. The houses became too small for any gatherings or soirées and were reserved only for sleeping and making things. Pleasure took place in the open air, outside the green, silent village, in places where tents, shacks, and gorgeous chalets were erected. The wheat did its best to grow, but the market for it had gone and so it joined the rice and the corn, which stole into the canal bottoms and tried to sprout in out-of-the-way corners. It was not long, however, before our village took a stand against this infiltration and forbade the planting of crops that might exhaust the soil in a celebrated law that enumerated these crops, among which were wheat and corn, rice and beans. Nor did the law omit to encourage plants with a long-term positive impact on the existing economy (on which, see the story "Sunflowers").

Some of those concerned with the development of the village during this period claim that this transformation created numerous victims, but I can assure you here that the number of those in my village who suffered during this critical phase could be counted on one's fingers and toes, plus the fingers and toes of the neighbors, and that when these bad-mouthers say 'victims' they mean those lazy peasants and riffraff whose capacities could take them no further than the sowing of crops which the village no longer needed. It is true that some converted to crops whose importance and necessity had become obvious, but many—and these were the ones who suffered—insisted on sowing cereals. Some of them tried to get around the law that forbade them and encouraged the sowing of 'fancies' by planting wheat clandestinely in among the sunflowers, and the authorities were obliged to strip the land bare, plot by plot, in order to clean the village holdings of every planting they held to be injurious. Some people they sent to trial: a peasant in whose field a number of lentil plants were seized was sent to jail, and a family was banished and all its members expelled from the village (Case No. 1033 B) because they had organized a gang for smuggling seed beans, and there was a number of other diverse cases which there is no need to enumerate here.

Such limited albeit significant issues aside, our village had nothing to worry about. The hostile forces retreated in the face of progress, those besotted with the toilsome life of the family were defeated, and certain individuals were brought low. Thereafter the village discovered the true path to happiness with none to oppose it and labored to further embellish its offerings and streamline its affairs, courting the neighboring villages by constantly sending out delegations to advertise and announce the village's new attractions in the way of the pleasures and relaxations available to any who spent a holiday in one of its luxurious chalets.

H.G. Wells says in his book *The Outline of History* (Book VI, p. 660), "The abodes of the 'harem' and of luxury were full to bursting with slave girls, dancers, jesters, actors, go-betweens, and guards, all clustering around the patrons and the rich, endeavoring to gain the favor of the guests—that favor which filled the nests with feathers, the coffers with gold, and minds with pleasure."

Outside the village, time came to a stop and refused to breach its walls, which must give us cause to re-evaluate the meaning of immortality.

6

We frequently find that we cannot easily depart from places we love, but feel a need to rove about in them. This is especially true of a village such as mine that is so well provided with the comforts of life, so decorative, so sweet-smelling, so fragrant with goodness, with color, and with silence, such a foretaste of Paradise, so much the longed-for goal of the onlooker's eye and safe haven of his heart.

Were it not that I do not trust many of the reports that have come down to us across the long intervening ages, I would have taken you through my village house by house, chalet by chalet, for it is related that its prince (or its ruler, or its mayor, or its sharif), on waking, would drink a glass into which four or five locally raised sheep had been squeezed, that he used to keep in the house where he spent his forenoons eighteen females, and in the house where he spent his evenings thirty-six more, and that, before the village's army was disbanded, he would attend the maneuvers of the night watchmen, watching from a tent festooned with girls. Likewise it is said that he never had an opportunity to set foot to ground, that he used to snack before sleeping on powdered hashish and sugar, and that he was just and honorable, loved truth, goodness, and beauty, and pitied the poor. It is also related that the prince, enamored of ingénues, set aside land that he enclosed and planted with trees and shrubs, then furnished with dens and knolls, and into whose tracts he released numerous young girls, so that pleasure, in this wild and licentious atmosphere, reigned unconfined. A writer or two attempted to study this intoxicating reality, but the keeper of the papyri indicated that their writings should begin with the observation that these events had happened in past ages, before the tongue of the village had been paralyzed, and when they refused he ordered them to be thrown out and to die in exile.

The noisy, raucous, oboe-tootling, wordless parties held by the village would end before dawn to allow the patrons time to bring their previously agreed upon pleasures to a close before noon of the following day. The silent satisfaction of desire in my village reached a point at which the very dogs lost their dogginess and were transformed into no more than cheerfully yawning animals which the foxes stepped over and sometimes even dallied with. The patrons and guests would sometimes take a fancy to the idea of kidnapping the girls off the streets, jokingly or in all seriousness or in an attempt to alleviate their boredom, since this brought them (at least) a kind of pleasure. When they were taken to the prince's jail, the prince's men would offer apologies and gifts to the accused and warn the beautiful dumb girls not to cause trouble in the future. One noble act that history has confided to us concerned a man who murdered his wife for having given birth to five male children and not one female. It is said that the man buried the children alive in an opium field, and when brought to trial for his conduct offered by way of excuse his fear that his house would be reduced in the future to ruin, an excuse that the judge accepted, awarding him compensation.

A Seventh and Final Section

Suddenly the historians, narrators, and transmitters of information stop. They stop at the point when the village was at the peak of its glory. All its progress and flowering, everything it had given to the advancement of mankind, is cut off, and we find not a trace of it among men's papers or on their tongues or in their minds.

Was the prodigal, luminous village lost among the tracks of a savage time? And if so, how?

But before we turn our attention to the various (supposed) ends that may have engulfed my village, let us pause a little at an event that was discovered, neglected, amongst the thousands of tall tales and lies.

It is reported that a man of haughty mien found his way into the village and remained for a time exploring its streets and alleys, its highways, byways, and chalets. The only thing about the stranger that surprised the village was his total abstention from its diversions, dance halls, and delights.

Its surprise did not last long, for they observed him measuring the thresholds of the houses and digging under certain walls, and the village followed his progress from beneath half-closed lids till some patrons complained that he was getting in the way of their diversions.

The village was then obliged to issue him a warning, preparatory to his expulsion. The man, however, disappeared. Then it came to the knowledge of the ruler that the man had come from beyond the Atlas Mountains and was on a mission on behalf of the jinn of that region to undo the spell and untie the magic in preparation for the freeing of the village's tongue.

Spies were able to pinpoint the place where the stranger from the Atlas Mountains could be found. A report having spread through the village that he had captured some of its children and was raising them in a thicket among the tombs, the village set an ambush for the man and, after surrounding the place, took him by surprise and dragged him from his retreat. Two children were found in his possession. The man confessed, awkwardly, that he had taken upon himself the task of teaching the two children to speak. To speak!

Reports circulated that the siege had run its course and that the sorcerer who had come from the mountains of the jinn had been brutally beaten and torn to pieces beneath the villagers' golden shoes and that the two children had been torn to pieces too.

And that the jinn, later on, attacked the village, leveling it and turning its high places into low.

And it is said that this did not happen, but that a fierce, icy gale attacked the village during the season of the khamasin winds, tearing it to pieces and obliterating it.

And it is said that a furious nation of imbeciles attacked the village and destroyed it.

And it is said that a kind of ant multiplied in the vaults of the houses, then flooded onto streets, highways, bodies, and dishes of food and devoured them.

And it is said . . . and it is said . . . .

But what is certain is that the village disappeared, or was wiped out, and that the plot of land that it had occupied remains to this day—a simple wet, black, barren spot where hornets buzz and insects build their nests, and which is devoid of any plant.

And when you walk upon its crust, you may, if you listen hard, hear voices beneath the ground mewing and croaking.

Once, while imbibing certain golden beverages in a chalet behind the Pyramids, a contemporary historian warned us that the village was still above ground. However, being in a patent state of intoxication, he couldn't say exactly where.

Sunflowers

It is no longer practical for me to report anything in my mother's words: she has submitted and hovers apathetically next to an abandoned oven, where she smiles genially at the army of ants that marches over her flaccid, compassionate body. Similarly, my father was found, the winter before last, wedged between the buttocks of a fat woman who in turn was wedged between two bricks. It is no longer appropriate for me to seek the help of the tongues of others in the telling of my story, not because those tongues have been cut off "like men to whom blood revenge is denied," but because they have fallen prey to a warm, wise sleep. This being the case, it falls to me to tell my story through my own efforts and mine alone. Has not the time come, my friend, for you to help me, so that I can go to my bed?

1

Even the king swore to his ministers and advisors on frequent occasions that sunflowers had an ancient and well established tie to our village, one that predated those former ages when tomatoes were bluish-purple in color, the week had thirteen days, the universe was lit by five moons, and the original directions, rather than being four, were only two. It seems likely that sunflowers found their way to our village immediately following Our Master Khidr's murder of an orphan and a cat and his destruction of a ship (or whatever), and that they came seeking wisdom, even though I always come close to bursting with vexation whenever I recall, out of the blue, that God has devoted His mighty attention to camels, palms, grapes, the youthful servitors of Paradise, sheep and goats, Lot, the houris, rulers, dogs, stars, untruth, bees, the Yemen, ants, fish, women, the cow, flies, the cave, the Fire, female adornment, snakes, poisons, murderers, the Prophets, wayfarers, robbers, He of the Two Horns, figs, milk, olives, the spider, and justice, and neglects (and deliberately too) the sunflower, that strong, broad, yellow flower with its candid, luxuriant green leaves that face east to welcome the sun and turn their backs and face west to bid it farewell, and that bend their heads over the light, inhaling charm, beauty, comeliness, and sublimity.

2

Setting aside the blustering of kings and their sycophants, we may assert that sunflower seeds appeared in our village in the aftermath of the assassination of an infidel slave and the dismemberment of his body following his success in curing a wealthy woman of mange, the seeds being discovered by chance amidst the trash in his hut, mixed with galangal, barley, black nightshade, and clotted blood. Certain bright people of the area who were students of the Invisible then attempted to reconstitute, or even invent, something of the treatment for which the infidel slave had become famous, but what they came up with resulted in a woman getting a tumor, a she-camel hemorrhaging, and a maiden not yet two years married having two ribs removed. Struck with terror and despair, the village became certain that its relations with the Heavens were imperiled and as a result the Heavens were obliged, to demonstrate their good intentions, to inspire Father Abd al-Guddus—he who could cause the very rocks to quarrel simply by ordering them to do so—to travel to the village, where he settled on its right flank immediately following the battle in which the people from the North Side annihilated the people of the South Side because of a dispute over the division of water from the canal.

3

The age of the sunflower seed blossomed during the era of Father Abd al-Guddus. He boiled the seeds with yellow wormwood and water in which donkeys' hooves had been steeped and used them to cure piles and belly worms, and he pounded them (the sunflower seeds) with fennel-flower seed and extract of castor oil and set the powder outside over eight sunny days in the month of Ba'una to obtain the elixir that cures the impotence of newlyweds. He dry-roasted the seeds, dampened them with vitriol oil vapor, and mixed them with ash from burned hair to produce the compound that exposes animal thieves. He fried the seeds in village-made clarified butter, dried them by the light of the moon, added sesame oil, and anointed with the resulting extract withered breasts, swollen navels, and rheumy eyes. He ground fenugreek with locust marrow and added it to sunflower seeds and clamped them in the dirt of the baking oven to produce pills with which he was able to halt bleeding and treat dropsy, envy, and jealousy, and he added to the pills a powder made of palm hearts, acacia pods, and snake venom for the successful treatment of the death of offspring, loss of teeth, and feelings of loneliness. Father Abd al-Guddus was also able—this being before a she-devil who had fallen in love with him forged a plot against him and set fire to his den—to manufacture from the brown-striped kernel-seeds of the sunflower treatments for vitiligo, menses, and palsy, for putting a stop to the rule of devils, for bed-wetting and hernia, for causing wounds to heal, for thwarting the schemes of enemies, for preventing the softening of the brain, against sodomy, the falling off of limbs, and emaciation, for prolonging intercourse, and for the prevention of baldness.

4

After Father Abd al-Guddus, however, sunflower seeds failed to find a caring heart. What they found instead, as the desires of the ignorant and the uneducated took them over, were frivolous hands, so that they (the sunflower seeds) had to face eons of decadence and anarchy, when storage bins spread among the mounds of the village, bins belonging to people endowed with neither patience nor knowledge, who sought to realize just one success or treatment—even of hair loss, or in forming a relationship with a single devil—and these mild-mannered brown seeds were compelled to slip away, under cover of the darkness of ignorance, to the fields. The first to sow them along the edges of a wheat field was a man from the North Side who was renowned for acquiring wives, fasting, praying, giving alms, and, from time to time, performing abominations. The sunflower plants appeared, tall and luxuriant, with broad yellow flowers with crimson centers. They stood on the edges of the wheat and fava bean fields, where they were subjected to the assaults of transient simooms and the snappings-up of donkeys passing on the highways. The peasants therefore planted many and employed them in this important function, for they often suffered from weak crop growth on the margins of their lands, bordered as they were by roads or irrigation canals. Formerly they had used eggplant or riverhemp plants, or amulets, to protect the margins of their fields from the hands and mouths extended toward their crops. No sooner, however, did the sunflowers appear than the peasants seized on them, first because of their fast growth, second because of the ease with which they might be removed, third because of the beautiful sight they made, and fourth because they did not corrupt the soil. Eventually there came a time when the crops of my village stood splendid, serene, beautiful, and bordered in the fields with these tolerant, august, and towering plants—despite which, my village had not yet (even by that period) discovered the true nature of the golden treasure that these plants conceal in their seeds.

5

The first to wake to the treasures contained in the seeds of the sunflower was a man who, devoting himself to the Lord, had become a member of the troupe of God Rememberers established by Sheikh Muhammad al-Sabbagh. Now, because this company prohibited abominations and the drinking of barley grog and fought the chewing and smoking of tobacco, whether molasses-soaked or leaf-wrapped, its members suffered from the idleness of their jaws while they listened to initiation ceremonies and sermons, being, the vast majority of them, men who had abandoned such indulgences but found nothing to put in their place. However, this man who had devoted himself to God and joined their band was able to detect, while cracking the white-striped brown kernel-seeds of the sunflower between his front teeth, an extraordinary and perfectly legitimate pleasure, the seeds having a light and homely taste that posed neither danger nor difficulty. He passed this discovery on to the other God Remembers, praise-singers, and individuals devoted to the promotion of religion and, just as the seeds now passed from hand to hand, so sunflower plants themselves began to move from the borders of the fields to their irrigated sections and thence to their furrows. Then an adventurous peasant went and sowed three qirats in one go, overwhelming the village with a flood of seeds for nibbling that turned all heads toward the sunflowers, while eyes opened wide to watch and wonder.

Despite this, most of the sunflower plants remained on the borders of the fields, a few only occasionally penetrating to a few of the furrows, for my village hates, truly hates, plants of this 'ignoble' kind, which can never be compared to corn, wheat, sesame, fava beans, or clover. We toil night and day lest a single irrigation period pass without these crops being watered. Men fall dead and feuds arise because one man's water flowed at the wrong time onto his neighbor's land. A bride's dowry is calculated not only in the amount of money to be paid but also in how many ardabbs of wheat she will bring. Social position and the ranking of those descended from the Prophet and other men of high standing are calculated according to the quantities of such harvested crops they hold in their storerooms; effort, grief, and sorrow are calculated in terms of what they cost by way of the collapse of, or failure to realize the maximum yield for, the harvest of these crops.

Nevertheless, the man who had dared to sow three qirats of sunflowers next sowed seven, and within ninety days was in possession of a harvest of nibbling seed that he loaded into a sack on the back of his donkey and sold in the nearest city for paper money. The village scratched its head, trying to find a way to view the affair as it did the fortunes of hashish smugglers and traders in animal skins—that is to say, with contempt, derision, or mockery. But the wholesale planting of sunflowers had another outcome, for my village thus discovered that sunflowers are good-natured, strong, tolerant plants that care little about their irrigation regime or going too long without water. They do not mind whether the land has been cleared of weeds or grubs. Birds and rats are of little account to them. Give them manure and fertilizer and they grow. Cut off the manure and fertilizer and they still grow. In these things, they differ from wheat or cotton or fava beans—those precious, noble crops that are harmed by a passing footfall, a gust of wind, a shorter irrigation period, a delay in the provision of fertilizer, an early frost, or an unseasonable rise in temperature. If you add to all that (and my village did) the efforts expended on obtaining fertilizer, plowing, hoeing, and the careful supervision of irrigation, you will not be surprised to learn that six qirats became three faddans and that the sunflowers leaped from the borders to the very centers of the fields, to broad acreages. They could be sown in winter, summer, or fall. They grew with or without watering and with or without fertilizer. Their beautiful flowers welcomed the sun in the morning and turned west in fealty to its disc at its setting. They paid no attention to wind, mud, crows, foxes, birds, or dust storms. They were transformed, rapidly, into seeds that might be taken to the nearby cities, the ones who sowed them returning with a swagger carrying meat, Cairo-style bread, oranges, chintz, headscarves, and handkerchiefs, not to mention cash in their pockets and in their wallets and under their pillows. They took no part in the conflicts over irrigation, the diversion of water, or the late delivery of fertilizer.

7

For a while my village left things up to those of its farmers who were willing to take risks, preferring themselves the labor, effort, and reward that await the believer for having toiled, sown, and tended. But the sunflowers cared nothing for this cowardice coated in promises. They swept through the village's land holdings and tracts, they leaped from field to field, over canal, drainage outlet, and dirt mound, inviting looks from the other farmers with their relaxed, confident flowers, telling the sun, with a nod, to set (and it would set), and quietly converting themselves into pounds that bought wheat, fava beans, meat, women, honey, and the performance of the pilgrimage, quietly converting themselves into jallabiyas and broadcloth vests, and neither alarming nor exhausting you, nor keeping you coming and going all the time, or staying up late, or on guard, or monitoring the demands of the seeds, the tax collector, or the government, but standing between you and those destructive, bloody conflicts dictated by the need to maintain honor, crops, water, and fertilizer.

§

Wheat, beans, clover, cotton, sesame, corn, onions, and garlic began a retreat within the fields, pulling back into seclusion amidst the golden, captivating sunflowers that stood erect there, verdant, unstinting, and noble, while love, mutual understanding, potency, generosity, ease, and brotherliness became pervasive among the men, and henna, perfumes, and cleanliness among the women. It now became an easy matter for a man to broadcast sunflower seeds in his field at any time and then ask his neighbor, should he see him or pass by his house, to water them; thereafter, he would lead a life of ease until his neighbor happened to pass by his house, or they happened to see one another, and he would be told to go and harvest his crop. There eventually came a time when it was simple for one man to manage the sowing and watering of a wide acreage and even to make agreements with the merchants of the cities for the marketing of the crop, without waiting to consult his neighbor or neighbors. Thus blessing, praise God, reigned unconfined, excising the greed from men's souls.

The sunflowers, however, loved honesty and had little truck with trickiness. If the labor-intensive crops had been defeated and had retreated to neglected corners of the fields, the houses continued to contain cattle, donkeys, and camels that needed fodder and greens, cleaning and dung removal, watering, hair cutting, and hoof trimming. It was not fair that people should become sensitized to the sunflowers and insensitive to these smelly beasts with their constant demand for care and attention. The camel was not more precious than the wheat, the cow than the beans, or the donkey than the clover. A compromise was therefore devised—that the animals should eat the leftover leaves and flowers of the sunflowers. The stupid obstinate beasts, however, took their lives in their mouths and refused to eat sunflower stalks, and requested that food—beans, clover, and barley—be imported for them from other regions, just like all the other household items such as bread, meats, ta'miya, and oils. The people, however, refused to remain slaves to animals after having emancipated themselves from pulses, cotton, and grains.

9

It became our duty to sympathize no more with the camels, but consent to the general stand the nation had adopted toward them. A camel ran away and no one bothered to bring it back; a mule and two donkey foals died; two buffalos butted heads till they collapsed and perished—and all this only provoked merriment in my village, which fortunate place wallowed in its velvet, its trees, its butter, its honey, its perfumes, and its money. The days of bitterness and toil were gone, never to return, and the pleasurable gatherings where people sat on benches, in foyers, before women, under the shade of trees, or surrounded by money brought their own enjoyment, putting paid to ill-temper, murdering envy, paralyzing jealousy, and making of each day a luxuriant oasis stretching for as long as summer's heat or winter's cold should last. Let the animals therefore go someplace where God would look after them, for we had no time for fodder, dung, cleaning, and unpleasant smells.

The people of the neighboring villages now multiplied among us, selling milk, buttermilk, bread, ta'miya, meats, and butter, while the people of yet other villages became a common sight as they collected the cows, donkeys, rabbits, and goats. And the fields of sunflowers spread and spread, setting siege to the date palms and the acacia, sycomore fig, jujube, and mulberry trees, and the more they expanded, the more money, pleasure, comfort, and blessing were deposited into people's pockets. The time had passed when a man would lose sleep, not over a field that had not been watered or a crop that was in danger of being plundered, but over a single ardabb of wheat in his granary, and there remained no justification whatsoever for that ruinous ardor that had turned so many of the natives of my village into addicts of the sword. They shrugged the rifles off their shoulders and took care that such duties should never hurt those same shoulders again. Clean, radiant, eloquent, kind-hearted, and wealthy were the people of my village, and the sunflowers seeded and sprouted and flourished and flowered, to dry out and be transformed into a river of happiness, comfort, and wealth.

10

It became a matter of fact that we had nothing but admiration and gratitude for this noble plant, the forests of which, unbidden and unbequeathed, spread like cancer, invading the highways, the slopes of the canals, and the banks of the rivers and which then, in no time, sent out advance parties to occupy the village walls, temple buildings, latrines, and ovens. It grew as does goodness in the body of the believer and with each new advance the village relaxed further and further, stretching out its legs, resting its back against the walls, burrowing ever deeper into the luxury of its bed. At first, the village used to perform the appointed prayers one by one; then it combined them all into a single prayer. It slept when it felt like it and woke when it felt like it, abandoning to its beautiful plant the role of waiting for or bidding farewell to the sun. It was, initially, unconcerned about those individual cases of resentment that led people from the poor neighboring villages to scale the inhabitants' walls in search of wealth. Neither was it concerned by the kind of deviant behavior that led an unknown individual to rape a young girl who was taking her ease before her brother's house. It was likewise unconcerned by those ruffians who lay in wait in the sunflower fields and sought to wrest the wealth from passersby. However, when things reached the point at which robbers were holding up the village's inhabitants as they sat in the streets talking, eating, drinking, or taking the air, the venerable village council convened and made its decisions, the most important of which turned on how to repel the danger posed by the resentful. It therefore delegated one of its wisest men to deal with the matter, and the latter was able, after discussions lasting a full seventy days, to reach an agreement with the scoundrels under which they (the scoundrels and riffraff) were given the guardianship of the village. That night, the village ululated for joy, but its ululations, if truth be told, were neither heartfelt nor profound, but mere sonant ejaculations from mouths filled with butter.

11

The rumors circulating to the effect that my village had had to seek the help of the Bedouin not only as guards but to clean their houses and sweep up their refuse now became upsetting. These were lies to which attention had to be paid, for my village had permitted certain needy inhabitants of the neighboring villages to help perform its chores in return for wages, a step to which Heaven gave its assent in the form of the exquisite sermon delivered by the village's noble sharif one Friday noon in response to the charge that some citizens had handed over to the strangers further tasks of a more sensitive nature that had to do with women. The women of my village lodged a complaint against this frivolous attempt made by a couple of youths (both notorious bean and wheat lovers) to raise a public outcry whose only purpose was to expel the good-hearted strangers. They did so on the grounds that those two youths, specifically, did not perform their prayers and that their hearts had been emptied of all mercy as a result of their long-standing relationship with a saboteur whom the village had driven out for attempting to get the fire going at a bakery, with the intention of attempting to make bread and thus fan the fires of backwardness among its citizens.

Horsemen Adore Perfumes

The day shuddered and shook the nests of the little birds into the furnace of fire. Grief jumped to the left and poured dust over the bodies of the children. The cities shook with laughter, hymns, dementia, and glee. The ovens of the villages collapsed on the pots of baking food and the warming bread.

A woman who loves dogs and collects foxes said, "Beware this sour black face! It leaves sterility behind it and spreads fornication. It wrangles with the truth, smashes silk cocoons, trades in the skins of virgins, brings sadness, and feeds on adversity."

❧

The day shuddered and shook the nests of the little birds into the furnace of fire. The ravens laughed long, till their feet and beaks and the tips of their wings turned white. The lower banks of the canals developed cracks where esparto, datura, and lizards grew to giant size. Ants pranced around the udders of the cows. The horseman unsheathed his blade and mounted his pitch-black steed. The children of the poor circled about him and he bestowed upon them

73

smiles and strength of purpose, solace and sweetmeats. The horseman pushed on through the throngs, the streets, and the sorrows till he reached the palace of the Enchantress of the Age. The weather was springlike, the sorrow warm, the sadness ablaze.

"Doltish and evil Enchantress of the Age, squatting on the village throne, I am come to take vengeance for your bloody gorging on the livelihoods of the poor."

The masses charged in fury, the trees clung to the remnants of green, and the waters of the river wrestled with the cracks of the drought. The guards clung to the walls of the palace, ready to defend the enchantress. The beautiful enchantress looked down from her royal compartment, and the people exploded with ire and rocks, screams and brickbats. The enchantress, however, stood her ground unmoved. The throngs increased in tenacity and solidarity around the horseman, whose smile expanded till it embraced the sheep, the waterwheels, the children, the ovens, the masses, the songs of praise, and the songs of patience. The horseman advanced his last step, determined to close the account of the bitter years. The masses moved behind him, carrying their children on their shoulders. The enchantress made a gesture with her arm. The crowds halted. The guards closed ranks more tightly, made themselves yet readier for the annihilation of the masses. And the enchantress screamed in her furious, tender voice, "I know your demands, but beware of blood. What harm have the guards and the masses done that they should fight one another? I am prepared to investigate the matter."

☉

The horseman advanced. In the forenoon the investigation began and in the evening the marriage was announced, and the masses were intoxicated with merriment and rejoicing, joy and exultation. And on the fourth day the enchantress emerged from her palace dragging behind her the body of the stubborn horseman, smeared with perfumes. She dragged him through the streets as far as the village market and in the middle of the square laid out the horseman's body, smeared with perfumes, and cut off his head.

Grief jumped to the left and poured dust over the bodies of the children. The cities shook with laughter, hymns, dementia, and glee. The acacias advanced, destroying the fruits of the mulberry trees. The braziers were extinguished and the dogs climbed onto the beds, the bedding, the seats. The snakes took their ease in the burrows of the rabbits. The hornets buzzed around the water butts. The poor gathered close round the bards and the storytellers, the chanters of collects and the concocters of charms. The bellies teemed with worms. The horseman's brother unsheathed his blade and mounted his pitch-black steed. The children of the poor circled about him and he bestowed upon them smiles and strength of purpose, solace and sweetmeats. The horseman pushed on through the throngs, the streets, and the sorrows till he reached the palace of the Enchantress of the Age. The weather was springlike, the sorrow warm, the sadness ablaze.

"Doltish and evil Enchantress of the Age, squatting on the village throne, I am come to take vengeance . . . ."

The enchantress made a gesture with her arm. In the forenoon the investigation began and in the evening the marriage was announced, and the masses were intoxicated with merriment and rejoicing, joy and exultation. And on the fourth day the enchantress emerged from her palace dragging behind her the body of the stubborn horseman, smeared with perfumes. She dragged him through the streets as far as the village market and in the middle of the square laid out the horseman's body, smeared with perfumes, and cut off his head.

꩜

The ovens of the villages collapsed on the pots of baking food and the warming bread. The mouths closed and opened and the saliva began to flow. The mind twisted to the right and to the left and then shrank back inside its skull. Sheep laid eggs, guts went dry, and rosebushes sprouted cabbages. Love jammed in lumps inside ovarian tubes. Broomrape teased the debilitated fava beans with lines of wisdom verse. An angel intimated to the Lord that He might wish to halt the farce. The horseman's son unsheathed his blade and mounted his pitch-black steed. The children of the poor circled about him and he bestowed upon them smiles and strength of purpose, solace and sweetmeats. The horseman pushed on through the throngs, the streets, and the sorrows till he reached the palace of the Enchantress of the Age. The weather was springlike, the sorrow warm, the sadness ablaze.

"Doltish and evil Enchantress of the Age, squatting on the village throne, I am come to take vengeance . . . ."

The enchantress made a gesture with her arm. In the forenoon the investigation began and in the evening the marriage was announced, and the masses were intoxicated with merriment and rejoicing, joy and exultation. And on the fourth day the enchantress emerged from her palace dragging behind her the body of the stubborn horseman, smeared with perfumes. She dragged him through the streets as far as the village market and in the middle of the square laid out the horseman's body, smeared with perfumes, and cut off his head.

The clouds drooped, darkened, and complained of the absence of water. The underground vaults writhed in ruin and extended themselves into the depths of the jugulars. The woman who loves dogs and collects foxes applied herself to homilies with the angels. The horseman's grandson unsheathed his blade and mounted his pitch-black steed and in the forenoon the investigation began.

A Woman

A few lines from now something horrible is going to happen: we shall release the notorious A to scale the walls of the residence of Mrs. N. He will then invade her bed, strangle her with his strong arms, and leave her a lifeless corpse, blood running from its nose and mouth and flooding the world.

As far as the basics are concerned, Mrs. N is beautiful and suffers from a conspicuous desire for unbuttonedness. One young woman has related an embarrassing and ambiguous story about her, a story later confirmed by the corpse of a mendicant cloth-seller. Also, a truck driver stabbed her with a dagger in her left shoulder some days after the departure of her husband. More recently, the tale has gone around that some swindler divested her of enough gold to fill his cupped hands, after which the reports about Mrs. N flowed so freely that it felt as though everyone had some story to tell of her.

And as though anyone might quite possibly have a story to tell of her in the future.

1

The winter was bitter and the low, narrow rooms of the houses whistled with shivers and cold. As the tea boiled on the open fire with its fiery red embers, our tales of Mrs. N would reach their peak, and when the smoke from the fire filled our eyes, noses, and throats, Mrs. N's body, house, and money would be plundered for our tales. Our smoke-filled, shivering-cold happiness attained its pinnacle when each of us artfully left a part of the story shrouded in mystery, so that we could delight in our efforts to uncover the details. One market day, the nurse from the hospital had been seen in front of Mrs. N's house. What was he doing there? Here the narrator would stop, rub his nose, and whisper, "Only God knows." The next would pick up the thread and insist that he had in fact seen her at the hospital seventeen days ago. What was she doing there? The storyteller would stop and whisper, "Only God knows." It would become clear to us at that point that we had all run into Mrs. N at the market, on the Bahr Yusuf road, in front of the school, above the barrages, at the dentist's, at the land-tax office, next to the house of the assistant mayor, inside the mill, at the train station, at the grocer's, in the graveyard. What was she doing there? Only God knew.

2

Daba, whose specialization was groping for the calf in its mother's womb and assisting its emergence, had rolled back his sleeves and was easing the last bloody leavings from the belly of a cow, when a one-eyed man bent over the careworn wife of my uncle on my father's side and whispered, "There are no real men left in this village."

And we all looked toward the place where we must necessarily assure ourselves as to the truth of the village's being empty of real men. Mrs. N was swaying at the end of the road, wearing her black garment that, as ever, undulated in the morning breeze and reflected the sun's rays, on her head a covering that showed to advantage her soft, beautiful face.

Twenty eyes laid siege to her as she stepped out along the top of the canal. This became the appropriate time for Daba to remove his bloody hand from the cow's belly and exclaim, "There are no real men left in this village!" The conference that convened around the aborted cow was quickly transformed into a meeting of solidarity and brotherhood in the denial of Daba's accusation, and in a voice congested with manliness the one-eyed man screamed, "I'll pay five pounds out of my own pocket to rid the village of . . ." (making a contemptuous gesture with his head toward Mrs. N). An unemployed man responded, "And I'll pay five!" A man of distinction screamed, "And I'll pay two!" A debauchee chanted in an ancient voice, "And I'll pay eight!" And the contributions echoed through the group until finally Daba's voice announced, "I will make an agreement on your behalf with Mr. A." The wife of my uncle on my father's side almost ululated with joy, proclaiming that she would slaughter half the rabbits she owned and hold a banquet of Jew's mallow in the street the day she heard the news about Mrs. N.

3

Just as every village has a tinner of copper pots, a school principal, a head of night guards, a thief, a drummer for the zar, a teller of fortunes from the depths of a puddle of ink, a seller of wormwood, an imam, a priest, a cattle trader, a marriage notary, a dancing girl, a house of ill-repute, a bone-setter, a waterwheel maker, a midwife, a mayor, a water-carrier, and a barber, so too every village has a hired killer who takes care of it and is taken care of by it.

Mighty A became acknowledged as the strongest man of his day, once our village had taken pride in his five killings — the assassination of a trader from the north at the behest of a blind woman whom the dead man had cheated over the price of a measure of grain; the stabbing with a lance of the bookkeeper of a neighboring estate at the behest of his predecessor; the beheading of a horseman who had been accustomed to pace gaily over the land without saying to people, "Peace be upon you"; the hanging by his heels in front of the door of the bakery of its owner, whom no one dared to release and who hung there till he died; and the fifth, when he killed a fisherman and placed him in a boat with his children and pushed the boat, ablaze with fire, into the waters of the Bahr Yusuf.

Needless to say, Daba it was who came to an agreement with Mr. A, and when they entered our street we all shook with confusion, excitement, and disquiet. Mr. A proceeded calmly, in his hand a rod of cane that writhed around him, anointed with glory and the breaking of necks. When he disappeared at the end of the street we felt vanity and pride pass through our souls, and no sooner had he left it than the mighty response swept through us that yes, this village was full of real men. Said A, as he proceeded calmly, "Upon you be peace."

4

Likewise, we knew when to expect that killings would take place in our village—in the morning, at dawn, or a little after the evening prayer—and were capable of discussing the murderer's wages and the method he would use to dispatch his victim—a knife, burning, poison, strangulation using the hands or a palm-fiber rope, or smothering with the bedclothes. Over the course of an exhausting week, we came to the conclusion that Mr. A would kill the accursed Mrs. N by strangling her with his hands, at dawn on market's eve to be precise.

5

Toward the end of the afternoon—that time of the day when we tend not to kill anyone—as the late sun, yellow, gloomy, and cold, declined, its rays brushing the melancholy of the rooftops, the village horizon was split in two and its eyes opened in alarm, its shadow banging to and fro against the garbage heaps of the waste lots. A terrifying scream rent the universe, Mrs. N's window burst open, and Mr. A was thrown out of it, to land in the street, pulling behind him that terrifying, drawn out, sequent scream.

Everyone gathered where Mr. A's body lay in a heap, shuddering and heaving with its last breaths.

But not one of us was able to raise his eyes to Mrs. N's window, for she stood on the roof of her house, steadfast, proud, and completely naked, looking at us with a smile of contempt.

The Edge of the Day

The sun, a little flustered, blushed a brighter red. A fox dropped down into the ditch and, once sure all was well, stuck out its muzzle from the midst of the riverhemp foliage, and lapped at the water. A frog poked its head up, causing the fox to stop drinking and ready itself for the hunt. The Hajj set his little, only, son in front of him on his jenny (its back dyed with henna because of its many wounds), towing his cow and its newborn offspring behind him. A mongoose peered out from among the stalks of sugarcane, hoping the traffic would die down so that it could cross the road. Two clouds moved close to one another and merged, their undersides spurting red, and an insurgency of starlings burst into the sky, creating turmoil and making the little calf skitter, though the cow continued its calm progress behind the donkey of the Hajj (who hummed a song the while and tenderly pinched his child's neck, teasing him and calling the boy names to keep him happy). The Hajj hit the donkey's neck to make it step over a fissure in the path, but the donkey bucked and the Hajj tightened his grip, hugging his son to his chest and almost falling off. He hit the donkey again, cursing the father of the one who had sold her to him. This alarmed the mongoose, which retreated into the sugarcane. On the other side, a jackal peered at the Hajj, his son, the jenny, the cow, and the calf, opened one eye, closed the other, and lay down. The Hajj asked his son, "Were you scared?" and the child cried. He repeated the question, "Were you scared?" and the child stopped crying. The Hajj swore to his son that he would turn out a coward like his maternal uncles and pinched him a number of times on his ear. The child laughed and the Hajj laughed and the little calf ran away from its mother and then came back to her.

The sun turned a yet brighter red and was forced to tuck its head below the mountain, dragging its shawl of light from around the necks of the palms. My aunt Nafisa lit the oven, sending the smoke billowing and the soot settling on the surface of the platters of fish set out in rows on the ground, their tops crowned with tomatoes, oil, and cracked wheat. The dog smelled the smell, yawned, moved along the top of wall, jumped down into the courtyard, and approached the platters, investigating the ground with his nose. Then he lay down. The rabbits belonging to Amna Umm Muhammad emerged from their burrows and spread out, their eyes glittering, and sniffed at the stalks in the dust. The Hajja felt the lips of the hens' vents to assure herself they were laying and called out to her daughter, reviling her for her sloth in transferring water from the earthenware butt to the jugs before night came. Mahmud Abd al-Jabir managed to secure his camel next to his door before smearing it with black oil to give it some relief from the mange. Sheikh Husni pulled at the sleeve of his friend Mahmud Hasanayn's jallabiya, tugging at him and urging him to accompany him to the mosque so that they could pray the sunset prayer together. When his friend resisted, Sheikh Husni accused him of disbelief, called down curses on his head, and informed him angrily that he would surely burn in Hell. A small group gathered around a jack and a jenny that had been granted an opportunity for mutual interaction, and Umm Kamil put the low table down by the men, at the entrance to the house, setting out on it a dish of Jew's mallow, a dish of taro, and two plates of bread heated in the ashes of the oven; then she called to Mahmud, her husband, to eat dinner. He swore oaths to his comrades urging them to come with him and share the food. Three, or possibly four, children made their way toward the kerosene vendor at the end of the street, holding bottles and eggs or corn cobs in their hands, and Asil's wife closed the sack of salt, asking a passerby to move it from outside the house to inside the house, refusing to sell the salt on credit with the excuse that dark was coming. Ali Hafiz circled Abd al-Mu'ti's house twice, gazing foxily at the entrance and taking care not to let the others see him and so disturb him in the execution of his desire. Sheikh Musa closed his Qur'an and passed his hand over the face of Adawi's son where he lay sleeping beneath the woolen blanket, calling on the Heavens to cure him and the angels to bless him. Umm Muhammad dragged a bundle of kindling from behind the house and put it in front of the brazier before heating the bread as an announcement that dinner was ready, and a little girl stood on the threshold of Sheikh Mahmud Ali Shinnawi's house asking for a bit of yeast to add to the dough. The donkey barber remained engrossed in his work in the middle of the square, and Sheikh Ibrahim called to Sheikh Ghazli, asking him to come down so that they could go together to a council of reconciliation to be

held on the North Side. Daba Abu Sami placed a pinch of
opium under his tongue and hastened to the café to drink a
cup of sugarless coffee, and Salah Ibrahim remained standing
in front of his house (which he had sold to Muhammad Abd
al-Mun'im and was now living in as a tenant) wearing his clean,
ironed jallabiya and savoring the respect of the passersby.
Badi'a Umm Sabri stood weeping and sobbing before Sheikh
Ghalib, complaining of her only son, who would enter his
wife's apartments, his pockets full of halvah and ta'miya,
by another door, using a route that took him far wide of his
mother. Abdillah moved from his doorstep and climbed the
stairs to the room on the roof, where he found his wife sitting
on the floor, legs exposed, sieving sorghum, and he started
to rub up against her, his eyes flashing. Shafiga stood on the
roof to hang out the clothes, heedless of the night's approach.
Salih Yasin and Ahmad Abd al-Aziz sat on the wooden bench
ripping the honor of one of the other families to shreds and
drinking tea. Khwaja Yanni passed on his way back from the
mill, smudged with white, and said to the people sitting in the
street, "Peace be upon you," and Muhammad Abd al-Tawwab
Ahmad hoisted his young child onto his shoulders and left the
house to go to the store and buy the boy halvah.

The sun grew ever more strangulated, and the underside of
the two clouds darkened. The fox, still in the ditch, sure of its
safety, slunk forward, readying itself to leap onto the frog that
was poking its head up above the surface of the water. The
jackal closed its open eye and opened its closed eye. Cawing,
a crow circled and turned in the air. The Hajj lifted the face of
his son with the palm of his hand to show him the crow, and

the child chortled with laughter. The foot of the mongoose touched watered ground and it took fright at the mud and drew back. The Hajj imitated the sound of the crow to add to his only boy's enjoyment, then raised the boy and stood him on the donkey's back and bit him on the cheek, so that the boy kept on laughing. The donkey sensed what was going on and slowed down considerably, but the Hajj shooed her on with his legs, the cow still calmly pulling her calf along behind her. My aunt Nafisa put the first platter of fish into the oven and scolded the dog away, and he got up and retreated a couple of steps, then sat down on his tail once more. Amna threw a bunch of clover to the rabbits. Sheikh Husni declared, "God is most great!" initiating the sunset prayer, and Abdillah picked his wife up in his arms and carried her to the bed and laid her down on it, so that the pallet shook. Amid the sugarcane, the jackal jumped and the fox abandoned the frog's head and slipped away into the riverhemp. Silence enfolded the world.

Remnants of light at the world's far west. Silence. All the sounds of the village had disappeared. Aunt Nafisa exclaimed, "Dear God, may all be well!" and Sheikh Husni started, floundering in the Fatiha, taking the worshipers aback. The dog howled and got to its feet and the rabbits shot into their burrows, abandoning their clover. The two clouds crashed into one another, so that blackness fell over the palms, the sugarcane, the corn, the platters of fish, the dishes of Jew's mallow, the taro, the rows of worshipers, and the heated bread, and the hens clucked in alarm. The dog howled again. Abdillah stepped back and pulled down his clothes, while his wife continued to gaze into his face. Abd al-Hamid the Barber stopped working on Sadig's head and looked at the horizon. Hajja Shifa's body convulsed and she felt a sharp pain in her neck. Muhammad Abd al-Tawwab Ahmad lowered his son from his shoulders. Mahmud Abd al-Jabir paused while greasing the backside of his camel. Mahmud Abd al-Rijal's guests put the pieces of food that were in their hands into their mouths and cocked their ears. The bottle of kerosene fell from one little girl's hand and the egg from the hand of a second.

The village's whole body grew still and its ears strained, pricked to catch the slightest sound on the horizons of silence.

Umm Muhammad whispered, "Dear God, let it be well! Protect us, O Lord!" and a shot rang out.

In shuddering alarm, Aunt Nafisa struck her breast and screamed, "That bullet killed!"

⊙

Seconds later, the village's scream spread outward, languishingly: "The Hajj and his son have been shot!"

Naked He Went His Way

The man's naked arm hung in the air in the entrance to the squalid house. People stared intently at every fissure and ant hole in the front wall in hope of seeing the expected serpentine movement. All eyes strained to examine the courses of the mud brick and the wood of the façade, the palm fronds of the ceiling, the cracks in the walls.

"My price is a pound."

He extended his thin, savage arm upward, as high as it could reach, till it almost touched the ceiling. Then he turned his head to face the people.

"My price is a pound."

A pair of lips smacked and issued a sound indicative of astonishment, and someone unseen threw out the words, "What! You think you're being asked to catch an afreet?"

The man's arm drew back a little. His eyes widened in their sockets, then closed. He lowered his arm, so that it hung loose like a rope.

"Twenty-five piasters is enough, paisano."

"A whole pound, and that's fair."

Then he turned aside, picked up a piece of cloth, threw

it into his basket, and tucked his stick under his arm, but everyone's hands stretched out to stop him leaving.

A man known for his attendance at councils of reconciliation said, "Let's come to an understanding, Hajj."

The man said nothing for a while. Then he blinked, threw his kit on the ground, and took off his shirt, revealing his thin body, brown as a palm trunk that has survived a fire.

"Succor, O Rifa'i!"

He took a step into the house, then made a stroking motion with his hand in the darkness. Silence seeped and spread.

"By the honor of the Prophet and the word of Islam! O miraculous power and light of the Beloved! Succor, O Lord of Might and Silencer of Assassins!"

The hiss lines began to course, and eyes stared unblinking, clutching at hearts. Suddenly, the thin, half-naked brown man was shaking and screaming, "Enough! Enough, accursed one! Withol, enough!"

Then he pulled back, turned, and whispered, "My price is a pound."

Eyes relinquished the darkness of the entrance and started to lock with one another. A woman recently widowed said, "Where are we to get a pound?"

"My price is a pound, Hajja."

Taking a pace forward, the woman replied, "Forget the twenty-five piasters. We'll give you a rub' of wheat."

Everyone murmured and someone told the woman not to interfere. The man's thin arm was still clasping the stick and his eyes remained invisible behind the thick eyebrows.

"My price is a pound."

"You think it's the first time we've caught a snakey! The village never goes a day without a calamity. What's so special about today that a snake should cost a pound? Say, 'God is one,' friend!"

"A whole pound."

Tongues continued to wag amid the crowd, which refused to give in. The brick-maker told how he'd woken up a few days ago and found a snake wrapped around his leg and it hadn't scared him at all. The bone-setter reported that his wife had killed three snakes on her own, and a man wearing clean clothes flew into a rage, told everyone to quit going on like this, and, approaching the thin man, whispered, "Twenty-five piasters is enough, cousin."

The half-naked man's fingers fiddled with his stick. He turned around once more and started walking slowly into the darkness of the house, his face to the roof.

"Succor, O Rifaʻi! I abjure thee by the Prophet, swallow thy poison and break thy tooth! I abjure thee by al-Husayn, rest and refrain! I abjure thee by Him to whom creation stretched out its hand and then slumbered! Succor, O Rifaʻi! Succor, O Lord of Might!"

The sharp thin hissing diminished and became inaudible.

"Descend, withol! Descend, accursed one! Descend, thou who brings corruption to the milk and verdigris to the cooking pots! Assassin, descend!"

The hisses rained down like thorns, shaking their bodies, and the stranger drew back in alarm. Then he leaped forward a pace and trained his eyes on the low roof of the house. Once more, he faced the people.

"My price is still a pound."

"I swear by bread, the man's a thief!"

The word 'thief' violated all the rules and gave a fierce twist to things. The stranger closed his mouth and his eyes and stood unmoved. His lashes bristled and clothed his eyes in darkness.

The serpent's hissing stopped and the palm trees stood by, like towering afreets. The crowd remained a silent, corporal wall. The stranger removed his drawers, leaving himself completely naked, but the mind of the crowd continued to cling to silence. None felt that anything had happened to cause embarrassment. Not one glance slid to his burned, charcoal-colored body. His fingers reached out for his stick; he broke it and threw it next to his clothes, and moved calmly, stretching out his arms. In a moment he had been swallowed up by the darkness of the entrance and he screamed, "Descend! Descend, criminal! By the life of Abu al-Qasim, descend! I abjure thee by Umm Hashim, accursed one, descend!"

The man continued to bend lower, his arms plunging into the depths of the darkness, wresting safety and tranquility from their hearts.

"Descend! . . . Descend! . . . Succor, O Rifaʻi! . . . Succor, O Supporter of the Weak! . . . Succor, O Omnipotent One!" And then, with extreme, apprehensive, slowness, "Descend! . . . Descend!" till that black astounding coiling came twisting over the ground, emerging from sunken depths, its black hood held erect, jerking backward and returning, drawing after it the savage serpentine body.

"I seek refuge with God!"

The serpent continued to sway, the naked man to make placatory gestures with his hand, bowing and pleading, while the hissing entered the skin, the palm trees, the animals, the crowd, the bones, the heart, the mind.

Slowly the man withdrew and on the threshold stood up straight. He looked at everyone and whispered, "Did you see him?"

He picked up his broken stick, wound his clothes around it, and threw them into his basket, which he slung over his shoulder.

He cast a short look at the crowd.

Then, naked, he went his way.

One Way Only

I reached our house before sunset, in a state of exhaustion and covered with the dust of travel. My mother opened the door, threw herself into my arms, and burst into tears. I tried to make her stop but her unceasing sobbing pleased me. That wretch of a pigeon-dung vendor—a man of no standing and of whose village, family, and even name we knew nothing— that worthless vendor of pigeon dung had sworn at my mother and cursed her and said that, were it not for a number of considerations, he would have smashed her teeth in.

And the men of the village? My mother said (trying to appear firm after her outburst of weeping) that they were useless and of no value. Sheikh Thabit had stood by and watched. Ahmad Khamis wrote verses attacking the man who sold pigeon manure and accusing him, in the most recent of them, of being a thief, a swindler, and a bastard. Salih Yasin took the man—the attacker—by his arm and tried to make him calm down, and the man sold him a large quantity of pigeon manure adulterated with dirt and the dung of other fowl. Your uncle Abd al-Tawwab started yelling in a fit and swearing by all that was holy that he'd kill the man, but the vendor laughed in irritation and paid him no attention and went his way. And your paternal uncle Abdallah was a government employee and couldn't risk his future by getting into fights.

1

As I changed my clothes, I got worked up, angry, and oppressed. I consoled my mother with a few words and went out to look for that wretch of a pigeon-dung vendor, that man of no standing who had sworn at my mother.

2

The sun fell in patches on the walls. The palms covered the village with shadow. Sheikh Thabit was sitting on the dirt playing sija with a man I didn't know. I called out a greeting and alerted him to my presence, but he made a dismissive gesture, his hand tightening over one of the sija 'dogs' in an attempt to move it. The other man protested because that jump was not allowed, being regarded as off-side, and he claimed that that particular move was explicitly against the rules of sija. "I would like to ask you where I might find the pigeon-dung vendor who swore at my mother and threatened to smash her teeth in," I said. "Wait till the round is done," he replied. I stood there for a little while, but the disagreement burgeoned and their hands abandoned the moving of the dogs to grapple instead. The dust of the area where the sija board had been marked out rose into the air and the black dogs got mixed up with the red. One on top of the other the two men lay in an all-out fight to decide the winner. I waited for a little while and then went my way.

3

Salih Yasin wasn't at home. His mother, who died a few days later, said that he'd gone to the market to practice his hobby of conversing with the women of the village, an occupation that provided him with the greatest pleasure. Salih Yasin also died a few days later.

4

It was Ahmad Khamis in person who received me. He talked to me for a while about Sa'd Zaghlul, al-Manfaluti, Ahmad Shawqi, al-Mutanabbi, and Kafur. "What happened between my mother and the pigeon-dung vendor?" I asked. He nodded his head, took some papers out of a chest by the window, leaned back, and looked at me. Then, heaving a deep sigh, he said, "Listen."

"Yes?" I said.

He continued, reading from his papers,

They seized the pen of reed and waged war on the unbeliever
And fought him. The blood of our womenfolk is ancient!
The conceited good-for-nothing assaulted a lady
With varlet's words and . . . .

I interrupted him in annoyance. "Tell me what happened!" I said.

He looked at me sternly, and I came to the bitter realization that I was battling a whirlwind. So be it. But I still wanted to know what had happened and where I might find the pigeon-dung vendor . . . .

He threw his papers aside and rebuked me: "Appropriate behavior and good taste dictate that you should not interrupt

someone when he is speaking." I told him that the matter—
that a stranger of no worth should attack a woman who had
committed no fault, swear at her, and call her an idiot—was of
special moment for me and that I would like to meet the man,
for the woman in question was, before all else, my mother.

I stood in the doorway and he continued to look at me
with his bloodshot eyes, manufacturing an expression of
discernment and condescension. Shaking his head he said,

The ignorance of the ignorant o'ercomes me
Yet I the discerning o'ercome when we do battle!
Such are men's natures in these days when the lion by
ignoble fowl
Is fetter'd and the master's become his canine's chattel!
Who wrestles with the king of beasts a while
Surely must be cast down with a death rattle!

5

The cemetery separates my village from the buses, the train
station, and the agricultural road that leads to the capital.
I trod the dust on the ground that contains the remnants
of the bones of all those who have departed the village.
The thorns, tree branches, dry palm fronds, cactus, rocks,
and grave markers greatly impeded my progress. Sheikh
Muhammad al-Sabbagh lives at the northern end of the
graves. The door was open and Sheikh al-Sabbagh was asleep
and snoring. The smell of silence, fear, and death enveloped
the place.

Sheikh al-Sabbagh moved before I could speak. He opened
his eyes, which looked like two patches taken from his
patched clothes.

I put my hand in his and kissed it. A feeling of comfort enveloped me.

"Where might I find the pigeon-dung seller?"

"What is his name?"

"I don't know."

He pulled me by my clothes and sat me next to an earthenware water butt round which hornets were buzzing. He continued to stare at me inquiringly, his hands grasping the front of my clothes. He rested his back against the wall. He left me. He didn't smile. He didn't speak. He didn't open his mouth. He withdrew his arm and placed it beneath his head and slept.

6

Yasmin, black as the night, lithe as a pomegranate branch, ancient as sorrow, brazen as a dancing girl, casts the divining shells and tells fortunes, teasing the men and making open, raucous fun of them. She was sitting under the thick, bare mulberry tree in the village market.

"Cross my palm with silver . . . !"

I threw the 'silver' down among the male and female shells, after the customary 'whispering' with the spirits. Yasmin, playing with her shells, kept talking and yelling and bobbing her head and pointing without my understanding anything. I reached out my hand to where the fortune-telling shells lay, gathered up everything that was there, wrapped them all in a handkerchief, set them aside, and yelled, "Yasmin!"

Taken by surprise, she answered, "Yes?"

"Where might I find the pigeon-dung vendor?"

"Which one?"

"I don't know."

She said nothing for a while and then whispered, "Only three pigeon-dung vendors come to your village. One comes in the summer at the end of the wheat and we are not at the end of the wheat, and one comes in the cotton season, and we are not in the cotton season, and the third comes at any time and you may meet with him, by coincidence, in any place."

"Yasmin."

"Yes?"

"I want to know where the pigeon-dung vendor lives."

"Do you know anything of the villages of al-Ghurub?"

"I have heard of them."

"There, at al-Ghurub, on the edge of the desert, at Naj' Abu Karim, Saw, Amshul, Dashlut—don't bother with all those. After Naj' Abu Karim you may find a place where the Bedouin pitch their tents. All the sellers of pigeon manure live in that place."

"But I want to know the name of the pigeon-dung vendor."

"Your village is not accustomed to know the names of the strangers who practice their trades within it—the sellers of henna, wormwood, pigeon manure, and spices, the gypsies, the ape-leaders, the donkey-barbers, the camel-cauterizers, the hide-traders, or the vendors of knives, scissors, and sickles."

"And am I supposed to go to this miserable hamlet and stand in the midst of its people and shout, 'Which of the vendors of pigeon manure is the one who swore at my mother and slighted her and threatened to smash her teeth in?'"

"Is there any other way?"

7

From Banub, behind the mountain, to Kudya-of-the-Muslims and Kudya-of-the-Christians and Biblaw, and from there to Amshul, Saw, and Dashlut, and from there . . . . As I was standing at the crossroads, a heavy hand fell on my shoulder.

After the first surprise I felt that his face was not unfamiliar. "Welcome!" "Welcome!" He stroked his mustache and whispered to me loudly, "A stranger!" He put his hand on my shoulder. A thick mustache and wrinkled face. He was enveloped in colorful clothes, but friendly and cheerful. "So you're looking for the pigeon-dung vendor who has no standing but who attacked your mother and swore at her and called her an idiot." He stuck yet closer to me and I felt a yet stronger sense of tranquility. "I'm Ibrahim Shihab." "Welcome!" I said again and we started to laugh. He told me that he would like to be of service to me. My heart fluttered and beat harder and I felt anxiety and confusion, fear and apprehension. Camphor trees cover the area and the crows were making merry on their branches. On the right was a ditch of stagnant water and on the left esparto grass teeming with insects. He told me he knew all the men and women of the pigeon-dung vendors' hamlet and that he often performed disgraceful acts with their women. He said that he advised me to go back and leave matters to him. Then he told me there was no need for me to be afraid of him because he had no desire to do violence to one such as myself who possessed nothing, and he smiled. I told him that I was not able to forget that a strange man had done the violence of improper words to my mother. His smile widened and he took hold of me by the arm underneath a camphor tree and pressed down on me to make me sit. His eyes shone with intelligence and did not inspire feelings of tranquility. I told him to let me alone to finish my mission. He pulled me toward him with wicked vehemence and screamed at me, "Don't you know me?" I didn't answer, but my shaking increased. He said, "I am Ibrahim Shihab.

Haven't you heard of me? Do you not know that the area in which you are walking is one over which my influence extends in full? Give me money and I will cut the throat of any vendor of pigeon manure you desire." I told him I didn't have money. He struck me hard on the face. "The penniless aren't worth the dry leaves on the trees," he said. The fires of anger ignited within me and, standing, I distanced myself from him. Then I was about to run, but he seized me by the hand and pulled me toward him. The emptiness rang with silence and the sound of gentle winds; the rustling of loneliness shook me. I tried to regain my distance but he kept hold of my hand. "You are from an accursed village whose every inhabitant believes he is God's shadow on earth. Its men believe that they are a clan of the tribe of Abu Zayd al-Hilali. Years ago they slighted me in the village market, and before that a beautiful woman gashed my head open because I tried to seduce her, as though she were of the line of Imam Ali. I have been nice to you so you must be nice to me." I was boiling with rage and refused to understand what he was saying. I resisted him, so he struck me again, with the bitterness of desperation. My limbs moved so that my arms might strike him hard on the head but the wretch returned to my body and clasped it to him. He threw me to the ground and cast his clothes aside. He beat me till I fainted. He stripped me of my clothes and tossed them in the stagnant watercourse. He threw me over his shoulder and passed with me over the farmlands, watercourses, and sand dunes that border the valley. I was helpless, silent, and sad, and he was savage, furious, and taut. He continued through the sand dunes till he overlooked a hillock at whose foot were a number of tents.

He looked at the tents. He motioned to me to walk behind him, but I could not. He picked me up—naked, a corpse, sad, unconscious—put me over his shoulder, and carried me till we reached the place where the tents were pitched.

The men and women gathered around us as we crossed the settlement.

"O sellers of pigeon manure! O most wretched of this area! O you who have no standing! One of you swore at the mother of this man and I wish you to hand him over to me that I may cut off his head."

And he threw me hard onto the ground and placed his foot on my neck.

The J-B-Rs

๑ The voice of the J-B-Rs quivered with sorrow. The Great Jabir, laid out in his winding sheet, indicated to them with a blink of his eyelids that they should sit. One of them whispered through his tears, "Impart to us your last words, Father!" But the Great Jabir continued to stare into the distance in silence.

๑ Quaveringly, the voice of the clan of Jabir rose in a hymn that spoke of a vizier who started life in a pit. But the Great Jabir continued to stare into the distance in silence.

๑ Someone with a ringing voice chanted the tale of the one who was afflicted in his body by ulcers and whose wife carried him to the ends of the earth in search of a cure. But the Great Jabir continued to stare into the distance in silence.

๑ The faces of the J-B-Rs leaped from the corner to the ceiling, to the bedding, and finally to the face of the Great Jabir, which radiated light: "Impart to us your last words, Father!"

۞   And before the Great Jabir's eyelashes closed, he whispered forcefully, "My final counsel to you is, 'Get a camel!'"

1

A camel! And the delegations of mourners muttered, in patience and in solace, "The Lord taketh and the Lord giveth." Never had the J-B-Rs thought of a camel. One Great Jabir presided over the obsequies of another Great Jabir, and the camel roamed about, an idea that pressed down upon them as it materialized, seeping from those words of final counsel into their whispers, and every short while the mouth of one Jabir would approach the ear of another Jabir to whisper, "The Lord taketh and the Lord giveth," for as long as four-legged animals had been four-legged animals, the settlement of the Jabir clan had loved donkeys—had loved riding donkeys, shaving donkeys' hair, staining donkeys with henna, bridling donkeys, trimming donkeys' hooves, fashioning saddles and manure sacks for donkeys, doctoring donkeys' backs, and fighting sores, broken knees, and hoof rot—and there wasn't a Jabir on the face of the earth who could not tell, at a glance, the sex and age of any donkey, the number of shoes it had worn out, its hometown, and the trials and tribulations that had befallen it from the days when its hooves were still soft. The Lord taketh and the Lord giveth. A camel! Scarcely had the funeral broken up before half the J-B-Rs were convinced that Jubran the Stylite had lived thirty-five years as an ascetic and recluse on top of a pillar because the settlement was devoid of camels. A towering, imposing camel! Camels traversed the desert, carrying bread and fuel, patience and potency, to the isolated monks. Saint Garapamon had sought shelter from the midday heat in the shadow of his camel and then had slaughtered it from hunger, and the camel had wept in consent. The other half of the J-B-Rs convinced themselves that they were not like the Sons of Abd al-Capricious, who had devoted their lives to the goat, or like the Clan of the Cleidonians, who roamed the settlements repairing the locks of doors, and nor would they, from that day on, be like those notorious groups that had fallen prey to the attractions of chickens or rabbits, of peering into the future through puddles of ink, of beating drums at zar ceremonies, making amulets, and stealing shrouds from the dead, of grinding scissors and knives. A camel! Praise be, to the Lord first, and to the dear departed Jabir second!

The first camel, coming from Suakin, Samalut, the Forty-Day Road, or Siwa, appeared. With its high hump and towering neck, its head that gazed at the clouds, it towered over the settlement, and its voice, which resembled that of water gushing from a narrow-necked jug, flowed forth, calm and patient, as it slowly proceeded, placing its feet carefully to spare the ground. A wave of joy passed over the J-B-Rs and they jived and jumped, each higher than the last. A Jubayr clung to the high neck, while a Jubran climbed up the camel's hump but fell off and a Jubrana played with its short tail, so that the settlement grew in merriment and the Jabir clan swayed with energy and bliss. With every passing day, more camels made their way to the settlement, and with each new camel the J-B-Rs discovered meat, pride, and camel hair, and how much they'd suffered inside those pokey houses in their pokey alleys. So the J-B-Rs demolished the doorposts of the houses and widened them, and they strewed sand in the courtyards and plazas. A Jubayra invented a spindle which, though it made everyone laugh, produced thread from camel hair, and in the end she gathered these threads and made a scarf to go round the neck of her Jubran. Another resourceful Jabbur put together a loom and the settlement filled with camel-hair mantles, scarves, blankets, and warmth. An aged Jabara taught the young ones how to make camel litters, and the settlement was ecstatic when for the first time in its history a bride was led in procession on the back of a camel; previously—during that age of which they no longer cared to think—they had transported the bride from house to house without that extremity of joy which now shone forth: a beautifully made and decorated litter, with the bride up on top glowing and glittering, the camel swaying beneath her! Shots could ring out and it would not take fright. Ululations could erupt and it would not take fright. Fires could be lit and it would not take fright. Camels could be slaughtered—for feasting and celebration—and it would not take fright. It even reached the point that those who had got married before insisted on celebrating their nuptials all over again.

Over the course of a few years, the J-B-Rs got mixed up with the camels and the camels with the J-B-R-s. The ceilings of their houses were raised and they took to wearing the silken shawl, the woven headdress, and the elegant slippers. They surpassed the Bedouin in the manufacture and exquisite finishing of camel litters, and they succeeded in discovering a new compound for treating the mange. They also grew skilled at preserving cured meats for months. Two Jabirs who lived next door to one another took to storing drippings and gravy made from the bones. A Jabrun was able to corner the market in camel hides and became an expert at marketing these in the settlements that lay scattered throughout the valley. A persevering Jabra succeeded in creating treatments for vitiligo from camels' intestines and for deafness from camels' ear drums, for sleepwalking from camels' hooves, for disruptions to the menstrual cycle from camels' marrow, and for increased confidence on wedding nights from camels' penises. Then a yet more persevering Jabra succeeded in drying camel sinew, which he pounded with burned camel hair and the grease from the back of camel necks, ending up with a compound for treating sterility. Thus the settlement grew in glory, luxury, and pride until even the bodies of the J-B-Rs grew taller and their necks longer, their voices mixed with the nasal sound of water flowing from narrow-necked jugs, and their eyes grew bigger and their ears shorter. Very soon, their lips had become cleft and their feet had splayed out.

    ൮   The voice of the J-B-Rs quivered with sorrow. The Great Jabir, laid out in his winding sheet, indicated to them with a blink of his eyelids that they should sit. One of them whispered through his tears, "Impart to us your last words, Father!" But the Great Jabir continued to stare into the distance in silence.

    ൮   One of them hurried to collect sticks in a bundle to remind them that in unity lay strength. But the Great Jabir continued to stare into the distance in silence.

    ൮   Quaveringly, the voice of the clan of Jabir rose in a hymn that spoke of a vizier who started life in a pit. But the Great Jabir continued to stare into the distance in silence.

๑   Someone with a ringing voice chanted the tale of the one who was afflicted in his body by ulcers and whose wife carried him to the ends of the earth in search of a cure. But the Great Jabir continued to stare into the distance in silence.

๑   Someone with a sweet-toned voice recited the homily of the camel that had crossed the wide open spaces searching for the killer of its friend. But the Great Jabir continued to stare into the distance in silence.

๑   The face of the J-B-Rs leaped from the corners to the ceiling, to the bedding, and finally to the face of the Great Jabir, which radiated light: "Impart to us your last words, Father!"

๑   And before the Great Jabir's eyelashes closed, he whispered forcefully, "My final counsel to you is, 'Get a mule!'"

2

A settlement pure as pure can be, of men from pure loins. How could it be that it had never occurred to them to get a mule? The moment it had finished receiving condolences for the loss of the Great Jabir, the settlement began to look askance at the kneeling camels with their huge bulk, their stupid eyes, and their twisty necks. One Jabbur whispered in the ear of

another, "The Lord taketh and the Lord giveth. Know what?
I can't stand the taste of camel meat." And a Jubran stood
on a parked camel litter and gave praise to the Lord, saying,
"The camel, as you know, is a beast of the desert and we live
in the valleys. And Jubrana's only son was ravaged by a camel;
we freed him—the pity of it!—from the young beast's jaws
in gobbets." Before their minds could even start to deal with
these painful memories, the mule appeared. Meekly it looked
down on them. Calmly it moved, as though coming from
the mansions of the moon. A Jubayra ululated with joy and
sprinkled flour on its dignified face. Love shook the J-B-Rs
to the core, and they fired off shots and sayings and words of
wisdom, and in every mule that arrived they discovered new
qualities and benefits: the prophets had depended on the
mule in their exhausting journeys to the highest heavens; it
had shared with the scholars of Islam their enervating travels
across the deserts of Tunisia, Spain, Austria, and Portugal; it
had carried books, flagons, and tents for many long eons. We
had never heard (the Lord taketh and the Lord giveth) that a
camel was capable of crossing a canal; likewise, we had never
heard of a camel climbing a mountain. Let us therefore have
done with the camel, and that without bothering to mourn
or appoint blame—for we were people of the moment. A
wounded Jubran yelled that they should fear the Lord and
let His creatures speak the word of Truth. Then, with voice
raised high, he burst forth, flooding the place with his words,
as follows: "Which one among us can forget the Affair of the
Oven of Jabrun the Kind? The J-B-Rs are kindly people but
this is a true matter. Jabrun the Kind was returning that day
mounted on his comfortable young camel, but at the turning
by the Great House the camel flew into a rage. It flew into
a rage and bashed against the walls and rushed through the

streets like a tornado, while Jabrun the Kind, clinging to its
back, screamed and the J-B-Rs watched from the doorways
and windows and laughed. Then the raging beast managed
to throw Jabrun the Kind off its back, only to kick him
against the wall, breaking his neck, and then went raging on
till it charged into the house of its owner and the walls were
brought down on the family of Jabrun the Kind and the camel
carried on trampling the place with its legs and its haunches
till the oven collapsed and fires broke out. And what then, O
wounded Jubran? Even then, the J-B-Rs kept on laughing."
At this point, a Jubayr silently rose, rushed over to his camel,
and smote it with his weapon as a demonstration of his
hatred for such an animal, and the settlement would have
turned into one great slaughter were it not for the continued
arrival of the mules.

❧

The mule found itself at ease in the settlement of the J-B-Rs
and applied itself right away to effort and activity, hauling
and carrying. Four Jubrans opened a cart-making workshop
and helped a hard-working Jabbur to become a smith and
an upwardly mobile Jabbur to become a carpenter, and the
courtyards, plazas, and compounds turned into places for
the assembling of the roofs, wheels, and shafts of carts. The
J-B-Rs were delighted when they saw their mules running
along the roads pulling the carts behind them to all the
neighboring settlements, and for the first time their own
settlement became acquainted with metaled and leveled
highways. Experts on the different kinds of trees, wood, and
iron and prodigies in the treatment of wounds, the mounting
of shoes, and the piercing of mules' abscesses appeared

among them, as did households specializing in saddles and stirrups, girthing and harnessing. Theorists undertook to direct the J-B-Rs toward the best ways of treating sores, leg swellings, and back suppurations, and the more the settlement pullulated with mules and carts, the prouder and stouter the J-B-Rs became.

The purity of the mule quickly had its effect on both word and deed. What sort of an age had that been when they had gathered around a jenny and a jack that were trying to mate? What kind of blinding crudeness had it been that allowed them to hurt their eyes with the sight of a she-camel pinned to the ground while her mate foamed and frothed with desire? Let us draw a veil over such memories and be happy for the J-B-Rs as they practice a refined life innocent of mating and groping about in wombs, of birthing and filthy wastes. Purity cast its shade over the whole settlement, and it became calm and biddable, earnest, enterprising, and generous with its wealth. The J-B-R clan became healthy, sound of incisor and molar, and none remained among them whose voice was repulsive like that "most unpleasant of voices," or whose throat produced resounding noise like that of water pouring from a narrow-necked jug. The mule was neither noisy nor disturbing. Its voice was smooth and delicate: neither a bray nor a bleat, but rather a tender delicate sound like a whisper—a mere whisper, incapable of rousing a man from sleep. Indeed, the J-B-Rs began to feel that they had never had a good night's sleep till then. Their throats shrank and their shoulders grew broad. Their noses lengthened and their withers and backsides grew fat. The hauling and carrying, storing, sorting, and trading had also, it seemed, put paid to that certain inherited desire for wife and sons, and it became easy for any J-B-R to go deep into the surrounding settlements for days and months at a time without feeling any anxiety or apprehension. Their sayings, songs, and poetry became free of the abominations of passion and passion-poopers, of betrayal and rapture alike. The vulgarities in which the ages of obscenity had steeped them disappeared from their stories. And very soon, the J-B-Rs had penetrated deep into the calm-cocooned world of gravitas, of wisdom, and of sleep innocent of the tumult of dreams.

- The voice of the J-B-Rs quivered with sorrow. The Great Jabir, laid out in his winding sheet, indicated to them with a blink of his eyelids that they should sit. One of them whispered through his tears, "Impart to us your last words, Father!" But the Great Jabir continued to stare into the distance in silence.

- One of them hurried to collect sticks in a bundle to remind them that in unity lay strength. But the Great Jabir continued to stare into the distance in silence.

- Quaveringly, the voice of the clan of Jabir rose in a hymn that spoke of a vizier who started life in a pit. But the Great Jabir continued to stare into the distance in silence.

- Someone with a ringing voice chanted the tale of the one who was afflicted in his body by ulcers and whose wife carried him to the ends of the earth in search of a cure. But the Great Jabir continued to stare into the distance in silence.

⊚ Someone with a sweet-toned voice recited the homily of the camel that had crossed the wide open spaces searching for the killer of its friend. But the Great Jabir continued to stare into the distance in silence.

⊚ A melancholy whispering arose, speaking of a truth telling mule that pulled its cart behind it without realizing that the cart had become detached and had fallen into a swamp, taking its owner with it. But the Great Jabir continued to stare into the distance in silence.

⊚ The face of the J-B-Rs leaped from the corners to the ceiling, to the bedding, and finally to the face of the Great Jabir, which radiated light: "Impart to us your last words, Father!"

⊚ And before the Great Jabir's eyelashes closed, he whispered forcefully, "My final counsel to you is, 'Get a pig!'"

Dayrut al-Sharif

Darwat (with *a* after the *d* and no vowel after the *r*) Sarabam:
A village replete with orchards and palm trees. The Sharif Ibn
Tha'lab erected a mosque there at the mouth of the Closed
Canal. It is situated in the middle of Egypt's Upper Region
—With minor adaptations from Yaqut el-Hamawi,
Dictionary of Nations, Vol. II, p. 453.

Dayrut al-Sharif:
An ancient village. Amélineau mentions it in his *Géographie,*
where he says, "The name is Coptic: Térôt Sarapan, from Saint
Sarabamon." Darut [with non-emphatic *t*] Sarayam occurs
in the *Dictionary of Human Settlements*, where the author
says that it is "a village replete with orchards and palm trees
at the mouth of the Closed Canal (the Bahr Yusuf), of the
Upper Region of Egypt." In Yaqut's *Names That Are Common
to More Than One Place* we find Darut [with emphatic *t*]
Sarabam as a tax district of al-Ashmunin, and in the *Laws*
of Ibn Mamati and the *Treasure of Guidance* we find Darut
[with emphatic *t*] Saraban. In *The Treasure* we find, "Darwat
Sarayam is a tax dependency of al-Manfalutiya, having been
transferred from al-Ashmunin," and in *The Triumph* we find
"Darut [with emphatic *t*] Saramam, which is Darut al-Sharif,"
and in *Dawn for the Night-blind* we find "Dharwat Sarabam,
which is Dharwat al-Sharif, from the Sharif Hisn al-Din
Tha'lab al-Ja'di, and it is where his house and his palaces are
situated, and the mosque that he constructed is there." In
the quadrature for the year AH 933 we find Darwat Sarabam,
and in the fixing of the land rents for the year AH 1230 we find
it with its current name, Dayrut al-Sharif.

The following names also occur: Darwat Sarabam, Darwat Sarabayun, Darut al-Sarayam, and Darwat al-Sharif.

All these names are distortions of the original name of Dayrut al-Sharif, which is Tarut. The second element of the name is a distortion of the name Sarabamun, who was an eminent figure among the Coptic monks in the first Christian period. Later the names were distorted into Saraban and Sarabam.

When the Dayrut police station was built in 1826, the village of Dayrut became its base, and in 1890 the place was named 'Dayrut District Headquarters.'

When the railway was constructed, the district and other departmental offices were transferred from Dayrut al-Sharif to their present location in the village of Dayrut Station, next to the station at Dayrut on the former lands of Bani Yahya; the distance between Dayrut al-Sharif and the station is approximately three kilometers.

— Muhammad Ramzi, *Geographical Dictionary of Egyptian Towns and Villages,* Part 2, Section IV

From the Secret History of
Nu'man Abd al-Hafiz

On His Birthplace and Lineage

No one in this world can pinpoint the year in which Nu'man was born. It is certain that Germany's Reichstag had been burned down as Adolf prepared to rid himself of the opponents of the Third Reich, and that Lenin had died and handed socialist Russia over to his obdurate successor. On the other hand, we find it difficult to credit that Chamberlain had yet taken over the reins of power in Britain, Greatest of them all, and it cannot be confirmed that my paternal uncle Mihimmad (so pronounced) had yet left the prison where he had been incarcerated for sowing poppies amid the cotton, which happened in parallel with the story of my grandfather, Hajj Mustajab, and the watch.[1] Thus we may close the parentheses around an approximate date for Nu'man's birth (and in so doing slap the hands of certain opinions that have sought to detract from our hero's standing), since it appears to be established that Nu'man was born on one of those days of intense heat when the summer corn is starting to ripen. For Nu'man's lady mother, who held a monopoly on the sale of salted fish along the winding shores of the Bahr Yusuf from north of the Dayrut barrages to the twists and turns of the Abu Jabal estates, bore him, far from the areas of high-density population, in her portable hut, whose movements were subject to the whims of the flood. It is also possible that someone assisted her in the process of giving birth, though this eventuality does not concern us. All that matters is that Nu'man was able, beyond any doubt, to climb halfway up a palm tree and swim in the Bahr Yusuf at the time that British tanks were surrounding Abdin Palace and al-Nahhas Basha was handing in his cabinet's resignation, and this agrees perfectly with, on the one hand, the reports which claim (in an account attributed to Sheikh Abd al-Aziz Khalil which we are disposed to trust) that Nu'man was born a specific and known time after 'the Troubles'[2] while, on the other, leaving us with the difficulty of ascribing a specific denotation to that word—the 'Troubles' of Urabi's uprising? Or the 'Troubles' of 1919? Or the 'Troubles' of the Ghuzz, who took up weapons along with the rest of the villages in this area in 1934, which ended when certain families abandoned their villages for mountain fastnesses and side valleys? And this in itself causes us to regard as unlikely other, highly dubious, accounts, among which is one that says that his one and only paternal aunt—the one who fell victim to rickets— was drinking tea in the house of the night watchman at the precise moment when she heard the news of Nu'man's birth, for tea, in the early days of its introduction to the villages, long remained—even up to the time of my uncle Mihimmad's exit from prison—the exclusive preserve of the upper class. Further accounts with weak chains of transmission include that which claims that Nu'man Abd al-Hafiz was born during the celebration of the Big Night of Sheikh Rabi' Musa Bilal, since, following a review of the names and feast nights of authorized sheikhs, first for the village and then for the area as a whole, and after discussions with their disciples and those who pray to them, we remain unconvinced that any such sheikh exists.[3]

It has thus become virtually certain that Nu'man first saw this world on the bank of the Bahr Yusuf in the period extending up to eight years after 1930, according to the strictest suppositions.

Nu'man's father was Abd al-Hafiz Khamis, a member of one of the clans of the Hadayda family established south of Dayrut al-Sharif. He was not possessed of property in the form of land, buildings, or merchandise. He did, however, have unique characteristics that made him one of the most famous personalities of the end of the nineteenth and the first third of the twentieth centuries, being an athlete who practiced the sport of running behind the donkeys of notables during their trips from the village to Dayrut Station, in hot weather or cold. He was taciturn and little given to intercourse with others, and this gave rise to rumors that he had expanded his sporting pursuits and had begun to appropriate small quantities of citizen's crops, nocturnally. People having thus suffered injury, they were compelled to search urgently for ways to catch him in the act, but Abd al-Hafiz Khamis, in his composure, left them no chance to carry out their designs against him. He soon disappeared from the village for a time, and returned leading a camel with quiet pride. From then on, Abu Nu'man hired himself out with his camel without respite or slacking, except for such rare occasions as the Big Night of Sheikh Abu Harun, for which he would wait impatiently and then, leaving his camel kneeling in front of his house, hurry off to the tent of the dancing girls, mouth open, face beaming. There he would sip hot cinnamon until, when the dancer passed in front of him for the twentieth, or fiftieth, time, Abu Nu'man's limbs would jerk into life and he would throw his felt cap to the ground and prance around her, dancing to the rhythm of the raucous, facetious clapping. Later, exhausted, he would drop worn out onto the nearest bench, take the usual coin from the pocket of his schoolboy's jallabiya, and throw it proudly to the girl, after which he would remain there, saying nothing, till the first threads of dawn.

One year it happened that a dancer called Badriya didn't give him an opportunity to go home after he had performed his customary duty, but stood rooted to the spot in front of him, and they entered into a powerful entanglement. Abd al-Hafiz Khamis continued to ruminate on this relationship till the dancing girl returned the following year, when he sold his one and only camel and spent his time following Badriya from estate to estate, hamlet to hamlet, city to city, till all news of him was lost.

Certain rumors, which we shall refute later on, made the rounds to the effect that Abu Nu'man was murdered at Muharraq Monastery during some Christian celebrations and that men from the village had seen his body with their own eyes. It was said too that the man was killed in 1919 during the celebrated attack by the villagers on the British train.[4] Then others with an axe to grind put out other claims, including one that he married the dancing girl and became a member of her troupe. It was also reported, retroactively, that Abd al-Hafiz Khamis repented and joined the disciples of a miracle-worker somewhere in the mountains.

All these libels were disproved when Abu Nu'man came home one year for the Feast—home to his village, his lane, and his wife, silent as ever, laden with experience and self-knowledge, but sans camel. He spent some time communing with himself, and then returned to the practice of his favorite hobbies, heedless of advice, indifferent to guidance, unconcerned about the Last Day, and causing his neighbors in the lane to get fed up with him, not just because of his conduct in the fields but because these rumors grew alongside an increased rate of disappearance among the chickens and young goats of the lane itself.

In the thirties, an 'Arab Council' was convened, Abd al-Hafiz Khamis was found guilty *in absentia*, and an order was issued by consensus that his departure should be facilitated. When the man, despite this, paid no attention to the council's decision, they set about doing injury to both his person and his assets. It was reported that they inflicted upon him the following egregious offenses:

1. A mad bull bursting in on him while he was taking dinner with his wife, Umm Nu'man, in the courtyard of his house, causing his eighth right rib to be smashed, for which event no one offered either explanation or apology.

2. Their collusion with the tailor, who stole a piece of the cloth from his jallabiya so that Abu Nu'man was forced to patch it with cloth of another color.

3. Their refusal to call on him as a witness in the case of the murder of Abu Idris, even though the man had been decapitated right in front of him.

4. Their conniving with one of those who remove snakes and scorpions from houses, who declared Abu Nu'man's house free of all creepers and crawlers. The next day a snake spat in the fish, and had it not been for Abu Nu'man's keen understanding, caution, and alertness, he would have fallen victim to their prank.

5. Their repeated stealing of his jallabiya, sometimes from the bank of the canal and sometimes from inside his house.[5]

Abu Nu'man remained patient and silent until his enemies exceeded the bounds of honor by proclaiming in the middle of the village that his stock of manhood was meager and that the reason his children had died before they had been weaned was that they had been conceived by methods repugnant to God. From then on things got more unpleasant until the sheikhs composed a poem against him that went:

Abd al-Hafiz, Abd al-Hafiz,
You whose ways are the ways of Iblis.
Go your way and leave us in peace!

and so on to the end of the poem,[6] which also contained an open threat to tie him onto a donkey back to front with his head covered in mud. Regrettably, the poem exceeded its duties as a warning and became mangled on the tongues of children and hooligans, who became addicted to greeting him or bidding him farewell with it, accompanied on occasion by rocks and brickbats.

Later on, or at the same time, the transmitters of these reports added a poorly authenticated tale, the gist of which was that one of Abu Nu'man's enemies had induced a rabid dog to launch an attack on the man's leg, causing him to lose patience and wrestle with the dog body to body, the general public assembling around them, delighted and uproarious, to laugh, mock, and urge them on, till both fell insensible to the ground.

The weak point in this story lies in the fact that the report of it only appeared in recent years, for it is an established fact that Abd al-Hafiz Khamis was bitten by the dog, just as he had been bitten previously by many dogs, without intervention from anyone. Similarly, it is an established fact that after being so injured, Abu Nu'man continued to rave for a long time and then began to have fits, went rabid, and became a danger to others in general and the residents of his lane in particular, which caused the citizens to become fearful of him and take precautionary measures against him. He continued to bark through many nights, creating feelings of danger among the populace and putting paid to its sense of security. Then news went around that some young men were lying in wait for him, and Nu'man's mother (who, it is believed, had not yet given birth to Nu'man) panicked and grew afraid and carried her afflicted husband off by night to save him and herself (despite people's assurances to her that she had nothing to worry about), making her way over the fields and across the highways until she became exhausted and could think of nothing better to do than to sit down to rest on a quantity of dry reeds (which were the very reeds from which she would later fashion her hut), and in that place, perhaps on that same night, Abd al-Hafiz Khamis died.

The strange thing is that the village that declared him an outlaw was the very same village that went out as one man to walk in his funeral procession, for the day of his burial happened to be the last Friday of Ramadan, and there is a belief among the common people that anyone who goes to meet his Maker on such a day is, without doubt or exception, blessed. They therefore said the prayers over Abd al-Hafiz Khamis at noon of the last Friday of Ramadan in the mosque of Amir Sinan, built by the Sharif Hisn ibn Tha'lab, a companion of Amr ibn al-'As, and it is said that the bier went round and round from place to place in the village and refused to head for the burial ground, and that the sheikhs pleaded with it to make its way to the grave but were compelled to bring it drums and pipes to make it happy, and that the women started

ululating, so that it became a noted day, for the bier dragged
the mourners along in its wake not just within Dayrut al-Sharif
but to the neighboring villages, the men panting after it and
pouring with sweat, and people of consequence got in touch
with the district chief, who brought his soldiers in an attempt
to bury the noble body by force, but the bier continued
to resist, dragging the chanting, praying, drumming, and
ululating masses along behind it. Regrettable disturbances
would have broken out between the people with the bier and
certain opposition elements had not elders and others with
experience wisely intervened, and had not the sun set, and had
not the bier dispensed its grace over the heads of the happy,
panting, exhausted people when Abd al-Hafiz Nu'man, finally,
consented to drive his bearers and mourners to the graveyard.
That night the village did not sleep until it had collected
money and the Arab Council had met in the courtyard of
the Amir Sinan mosque to plan the construction of a holy
tomb befitting the one who had worked this miracle. After
no more than four days (six, according to the version of Hajj
Muhammad Hasanayn) they had built the tomb, whitewashed
it, raised its headstone to a height of five meters, and drawn
on its walls horses, swords, ships, and a camel (a huge one,
whose voice could be heard seven cemeteries away). Then the
village gathered to transfer the remains of its saint to this new,
elegant location, strewn with sand brought in from the eastern
desert. Things did not, however, go according to the wishes of
the village, which had been trying for some time to expand
the number of its saints (of whom there were no more than
eight) for it became apparent that certain wild animals[7] had
scrabbled up the mouth of the grave. Horror increased when
they were confronted with a shredded winding sheet, while
the bones of the mighty sheikh, putrid flesh still clinging to

them, filled the grave chamber. The people prayed for God's protection and were dismayed, and left both old grave and new tomb empty.

As for what followed, it is certain that Nu'man was born immediately after the burial of his father the noble sheikh, and had it not been for the wild animal that violated the place (and we will make no attempt here to respond to the claim that was made, out of mockery, in this regard), many things would have been different. For there can be no doubt that a man who was dead and had a proven miracle to his credit would have been worthy of the veneration of the common people and that the inhabitants of the village would have looked after his son, honoring both of them to the extent to which they were able. However, Sheikh Abd al-Hafiz's miracle did not survive for more than a few days, and consequently when Abd al-Hafiz entered this world he did so on an eroded bank, in a hut made of straw where the winds howled, tracing for the newborn a new and different world, while the waters of the Bahr Yusuf, carrying the good news to the land and the fields, billowed on without attention to those dark clouds that were gathering over the world as it pondered the first signs of the Second World War (for it is said that, at precisely the same time, Mussolini's warships began to pound the shores of Abyssinia).

---

1. It is related of Hajj Mustajab that on his way back from the fields at noon on a Friday in summer he came across a round piece of shiny metal, which he then picked up, thanking God for His kindness. However, this piece of metal had two thin wires that jumped about beneath its glass covering and this dismayed the heart of the pious believer, which heart increased in dread when he brought the piece of metal close to his ear, for the satanic thing was ticking. He therefore threw the metal demon to the ground, uttered prayers for God's protection, and then pounded it with his crutch until he was certain that it was completely destroyed. This is a recent tale,

not to be confused with the one about Charlemagne's clock and Harun al-Rashid.

2. Faced by the large number of events to which the appellation 'Troubles' is applied, I had recourse to the piles of birth registers preserved in the district offices, which revealed the following: Abd al-Hafiz Nu'man is entered in the registers under the years 1910, 1929, and 1928. From my attempts to get to the bottom of this, it became clear that Umm Nu'man, Nu'man's mother, had four children. The first Nu'man died and she then had a second child, whom she named Nu'man. The second Nu'man died and she then had a third child, whom she named Nu'man, and she also named the fourth child Nu'man in the belief that the third was bound to die. However, these two Nu'mans survived for a period before one of them died, though we have failed to identify which of the two that was. The outcome was that Nu'man Abd al-Hafiz was called before the military service board in 1920 (when evidence was presented to the board certifying that he was dead) and in 1945 (when it was plain that Nu'man was just a child) and in 1962 (when it was obvious that he had exceeded the age of thirty-five and was "absolutely unfit for military service by reason of his having exceeded the maximum age, not to mention the impairment of his faculties due to anemia, which renders it difficult to determine his exact age." (Lt. Col. Dr. Muhammad Hasan Labib, Head, Military Service Board, Selection Administration, Asyut, 81962/8/.)

3. I have discovered that there was someone called Sheikh Rabi' Mursi Bilal who lived in the early part of the twentieth century, during the era of the *Pax Mursi Bilal*. He was not a sheikh in the ordinary sense of the term, but simply a child whose growth had halted and who had lost the faculties of movement and speech and who was visited a number of times by childless women and others with various complaints until it emerged that his powers were limited, at which time he was forsaken. He died without any miracles worth mentioning.

4. Prof. Abd al-Rahman al-Rafi'i's book on the revolution of 1919 does not provide any evidence of the name Abd al-Hafiz Khamis among those of the dead and wounded, in Dayrut or elsewhere.

5. It is also stated that they stole his shoes, which statement is to be rejected, on the basis of the non-availability of shoes at that period.

6. The poem is forty-nine lines long, and it is said that Sheikh Rashid, though a well-known chanter of the Qur'an, permitted himself the indulgence of writing secular verses that he recited on numerous

occasions, and some of these in fact came to be regarded in many of the neighboring settlements as containing semi-divine wisdom.

7. A rumor went around that what destroyed the sheikh's corpse was nothing but a mongoose, though some characterized it (without actually having seen it) as a ghoul.

On His Childhood and Youth

*T*he most cogent analysis among those who tend to treat the life of Nuʿman as a span encompassed by or linked, over the course of long periods, to those of other people (mother, grandfathers, grandmothers, paternal and maternal uncles) is that to disassociate Nuʿman's particular span from the lives of those who passed on before or at the same time as him should be regarded as an arbitrary act deployed by certain of his enemies with the intention of isolating his life preparatory to the diminution and, ultimately, destruction of his status.

According to this argument it would have been possible—on the Bahr Yusuf Canal, or in the very hut where his mother gave birth to him, or at any point in the incessant comings and goings that his mother maintained among the fields in order to market her goods (salted fish, halvah made from molasses, and summer dates)—for any low thief, wandering jackal, or stray dog to apply the dissociative theory referred to above and put an end to the whole business of Nuʿman by reducing him to a mere carcass, or the remains of a carcass, for the winds of the wide-open spaces to play with.

This was not, however, how things stood, for Nuʻman's eldest paternal uncle spent a part of his life earning his living by attending the Circles of Remembrance held by the Sufis and the gatherings of organizations for the celebration of the seventh, fifteenth, and fortieth days of mourning, and Nuʻman's middle paternal uncle (the one who had his belly slit open by a raging she-buffalo) was a specialist in the transferal of male palm-tree pollen and its employment in the fertilization of the female trees, and Nuʻman's third (and youngest) paternal uncle started out as a cropper of animal hooves and ended his life as a stealer of shrouds; and his maternal uncles no doubt had their own similar personal glories that no would-be deceiver should dare to treat lightly, even though the information before us does not permit any degree of certainty as to whether he actually had maternal uncles or not, Nuʻman's grandfather on his mother's side having been an expert in the castration of young goats. As for Khamis—Nuʻman's grandfather on his father's side—we have it on good authority that he expired on his pallet, which was stuffed behind a mulberry tree on the road to the village market.

All these roots combined to nourish Nuʻman's innermost being, as did the Bahr Yusuf, whose waters purled at the foot of the hut, and the towering trees rustling in the breeze, and a vast sweep of fields filled with green; and if we add to the scene a few birds in the air and a few lizards on the ground and mix all of that with the tributary streams of Nuʻman's original parental heritage, things become clearer. Those who have no love for Nuʻman have put it about that he received no formal education in childhood, though these theorists ought to elevate their ideas to take into account the fact that many children of teachers, army officers, government employees, merchants, lawyers, and politicians spend their childhoods in pedagogical crises of extraordinary complexity inside walls decorated with photographs of actresses, their families providing them with no experiences to add to their childhood memory albums more important than a few superficial cuts caused by mishandling a bicycle, falling off the back of a streetcar, or the collapse of a stairwell banister, since they rarely have the opportunity to climb a tree, or even play with a cat. Nu'man, on the other hand, whose allotted portion of education was zero, swam well at six, could swim underwater at seven plus a few months, knew at eight how to slip into the tomato fields at night to snatch the fruit, and, at nine, had got hold of a small kid and slaughtered it with a rusty tin can, was able to climb halfway up a palm tree, had smashed the skull of a dead dog, and had set fire to reed beds and a forest of cattails. Also, when he was eight, he struck two birds with one stone, messed about with an irrigation channel outlet and flooded twenty faddans and five qirats of land, committed highway robbery on a small girl grazing goats, stealing from her a cupped handful of sycomore figs, had been the reason behind the fall of a she-camel who was dropped into the Bahr Yusuf by a collapsing bank, had stoned all the (few) cars that passed along the nearby highway, and had pursued a hovering aircraft, maintaining, in a loud voice, a flow of insults against its pilot till he (Nu'man) fell into a fissure in some unflooded land.[1] When he was nine he knew how to castrate the goats so that the kids wouldn't expend their energy and fatness on suspect relationships. When he was ten he succeeded in climbing all the way up a palm tree, and dug a trap in the highway and covered it with plants and dirt so that he could enjoy the sight of the passersby falling in. Also when he was ten he repeated something someone had said to someone else, leading to three fights resulting in certain small calamities, and learned to spin a top and to play hopscotch. His first reprehensible act was to rob a man of his clothes while he was cooling himself in the canal. He also became known to the salted fish merchants in Izbat Shalgami, Dayrut Station, and Izbat al-Juhush, and collaborated in luring a stranger into a den in a narrow lane, where the man was killed.

It is believed that Umm Nu'man used to plead with him not to expose himself to such risks, he being her only son and her support for the future, and that she quickly became aware—immediately following the rumors of his involvement in the luring of strangers into dens—that the boy was much absent from the hut, just as she did that his average daily production of tomatoes, corncobs, and small fish had fallen off noticeably. It is said that his mother tried to question him, but that Nu'man, in contrast to his normal practice, talked back to her, nay, attacked her with offensive language, which I imagine he must have picked up from the local *hoi polloi*, and that his mother was compelled to strike him, thus breaking the rules of modern parenting though subsequently, repentant, she tried to make up with him. Nu'man, however, took to retreating into a corner of the hut and curling himself up in silence, then later to sleeping a great deal, and finally to hiding himself away for long periods and not listening to his mother's conversation or paying attention to her woes.

At this point, Umm Nu'man decided that she could no longer keep silent about things. True, he didn't seem to have a fever, and his lack of speech was a rest for her nerves and saved her the headaches, but she couldn't stand the silence, the curling up, and the hiding.

We believe that Umm Nu'man purchased incense, burned it inside the hut, and, picking the boy up in her arms, walked around and over the fire with him, chanting prayers and muttering charms to keep away devils—for harm had, indubitably, befallen her son, and the eyes of the village (dust in them!) must have directed envy against Nu'man, what with his energy and his talent for transferring much 'good fortune' from the fields to the hut. Thus did Umm Nu'man succeed in diagnosing her son's ailment.

Albert Camus, or one of those people, says that if you die this year, death will avoid you the next. Umm Nu'man, not being concerned with the sayings of Albert Camus, wasted no time but slung Nu'man over her shoulder and traversed the forests, canals, and muddy spots, treading on thistles and goat's thorn, harm and camel thorn, while Nu'man, over her shoulder, remained silent and unspeaking. From time to time, she would scream in motherly tenderness, "Nu'man!" but the boy did not reply. He moaned, all he did was moan, and so she continued to plow through the billows of the land till she reached Mu'ahada Bridge, and still Nu'man did not reply. She therefore persisted in the face of her exhaustion until she reached the government hospital building, with its cold cement touch, where she set Nu'man down and sat, then laid him over her lap while she rested her back against the hospital wall. Only a few minutes later, the hospital's doorkeeper pounced on her, and it seems that Nu'man preferred to respond personally, for the boy defecated and covered his mother in many things, the least of which was embarrassment. This increased the doorkeeper's fury and he commanded her to take herself and her ("filthy") son to the other door, telling her that it was forbidden ("God help us!") to sit where she had. In his fury he yelled that "these damned people" (one of whom was Umm Nu'man) would be his undoing and that the head doctor of the hospital would arrive at any moment. The doorkeeper kept up his frothing and foaming, asking Umm Nu'man to hurry up ("God ruin your houses!"). However, Umm Nu'man—being Umm Nu'man—did not take this lying down and, in a mighty voice, cursed every job and position included in the hospital's administrative chart, from the head doctor to the doorkeeper. People gathered and intervened out of sympathy for the hospital employee, but Umm Nu'man made it clear to them all that she was merely resting and would be on her way, and she stood up, heavy of heart, slung her hero over her shoulder, and crossed Mu'ahada Bridge in sadness and exhaustion, her heart pounding. "Nu'man!" she cried, but Nu'man still didn't answer, so that Umm Nu'man, at her wit's end, hugged him even tighter and set off once more, full of apprehension, her back hurting, across the forests and the open spaces, the dung heaps, the work camps of the brick makers, and the swamps. "Nu'man!" she cried again, but Nu'man still didn't answer, and she continued, her feet trampling rocks, thistles, and mud, until she had brought him back to the village.

Once among the lanes of the village, she turned right away to the house of Sheikh Abd al-Waddud, the village's secret and its protector, the bridler of its demons and reliever of its pains, and no sooner had she entered than the man appeared before her, uttering the words "In the name of God the Merciful, the Compassionate" and "There is no power and no strength but in God."

"All's well?" he asked.

"Open the door to us, Master!"

The sheikh extended his magical hand to where the head of Nu'man lay, drowning in stillness and silence, and the holy verses poured forth, hovering and filling the room. He drew closer to Nu'man and his breath, inflated with the miraculous verses, wreathed themselves about the boy's head, nape, neck, and body. Then he brought his mighty book, bound in ancient flannel, and spent some time turning the pages, reading, stroking the boy, and seeking the protection of God.

Suddenly, as though Sheikh Abd al-Waddud had seized the start of the thread, he fell silent for a moment, then gave his ringing shout, took up his quill pen and his papers, and began to write in violet ink with a penetrating smell. He lit a fire and, gently and with dignity, lifted Nu'man's body. Smoke filled the place and their eyes flooded with tears. "In the name of God the Merciful, the Compassionate," recited the Sheikh. "*O Company of Jinn, You have seduced many humans.*[2] *We said, O Dhu al-Qarnayn, you may choose which of them to punish or show kindness to.*[3] *We said, Fire be cool and safe for Ibrahim.*[4] *We have told you the truth, so do not despair.*[5] *But if evil touches him he loses all hope and becomes despondent.*[6] *Whoso blinds himself to the remembrance of the All-merciful, to him we assign a Satan for comrade.*[7] God has spoken truly, He is the Curer, He is the Kind, the Forgiving, that will be twenty piasters, Hajja." "Twenty piasters!?" But before she could honor his request, he had ordered her to pick up her son and step over the fire with him seven times and, at that moment, Nu'man coughed. Nu'man coughed and yelled, a feeble yell but audible. The afreet was exiting the body, the devils were leaving the marrow, the jinn were parting from Nu'man the Mighty, and Sheikh Abd al-Waddud inserted the amulet under Nu'man's armpit, rested his back against the wall, and stayed there, staring into space. Or waiting.

Here I would like to emphasize the extraordinary effort that Umm Nu'man had never flagged in exerting. Verily, many things in our lives are worthy of sacrifice, including, without a doubt, Nu'man.

Umm Nu'man paid the twenty piasters.

And she began to feel easy in her mind that her son would enter his adolescence healthy and strong.

---

1. There is a trustworthy account of the reasons for Nu'man's habit of chasing aircraft, which is that a kite snatched Nu'man in his first year, while he was lying quietly in his swaddling bands at the bottom of a dry canal; that the kite, scared off by the terrible scream released by Umm Nu'man, was unable to complete its mission; and that Nu'man suffered from bloody wounds to his right temple and left arm that did not heal for many long months thereafter. We have deliberately overlooked this incident, as it occurs in similar form in Dr. Ahmad Ukasha's book on Leonardo Da Vinci.
2. Qur'an, Surat al-An'am, 128.
3. Qur'an, Surat al-Kahf, 86.
4. Qur'an, Surat al-Anbiya', 69.
5. Qur'an, Surat al-Hijr, 55.
6. Qur'an, Surat Fussilat, 49.
7. Qur'an, Surat al-Zukhruf, 36.

On Perdition

e must pause now before the calumny—which is to say, the lie—that some swindler has put about concerning Nu'man, accusing me of having been party to the expunging of Nu'man's father from existence so that I could give the son the opportunity to grow to manhood as an orphan and thus prepare the way for his inclusion in the lists of prodigy performers and miracle workers. This swindler has documented his patent slander by providing the names of a number of famous orphans who altered the course of history, and he has even had the gall, this swindler, to invoke the case of a certain person who didn't even have a father to begin with.

We do not claim to be competent enough to score a victory upon entering the world of those upon whom the heavens have bestowed their protection. Nevertheless, a sudden insight on the part of a friend' who is endowed with a certain fleeting intelligence makes the point against us that most of us are orphans even when the father is present, and that fathers—in general and without denying the exceptions—are to be entered under the heading of 'impediments' (despite which you are still prohibited from saying "Ouff!" to them).

I hope to make it clear, when setting out the slanderer's calumny and the insight of the one of transient intelligence (while not completely convinced by either), that the early clearing of a father from Nu'man's path is simply easier for me than having him grow up under the aegis of a man whom I would, unavoidably, have to force him to get rid of by means which Heaven tends to condemn. I am able to guarantee protection to Nu'man from jackals, sheikhs, kites, the sick, politicians, snakes, culture, ghosts, teachers, burglars, the Bahr Yusuf, and scorpions, but I would probably fail to protect him from a father possessed of a not insignificant degree of kindness, patience, good temper, nobility, and gentleness.

The business — the business, that is, of Nu'man — was taken care of in just the same manner as are those of the wind, of evil, of procreation, of clouds, of honor, of fear, of grace, of the sun, of good fortune, of the stars, of love, of the moon, of courage.

Thus, at the beginning of the Bahr Yusuf flood,[2] Umm Nu'man started striking deals for the provisioning of women in easy circumstances and possessed of certain inflammable tastes, for whom she had kept in reserve a quantity of aged rashal,[3] the kind whose piercing, putrid smell you can detect at a distance of twenty qasabas, and one of the wealthy women of the village's North Side, following exploratory discussions that lasted through five such deals, unburdened herself into Umm Nu'man's ear of a virtuous desire, which was that the latter should grant her permission to purchase Nu'man.

It is most upsetting to have to lure Nu'man into abandoning the fields and the trees, the gushing of the water, and the pursuit of birds and lizards to go live in a village crowded with walls, contentiousness, gossip, deception, weddings, the distillation of grapes, and secret liaisons. Indeed, this constitutes a cruel blow to my soul and a massive disturbance of the parallelism of the lines within which I had wished Nu'man would live, even if the wealthy woman was the distinguished, majestic, Madame Fawqiya, she of the glorious pedigree, of the land, the dogs, and the two slaves, of the high reputation, the material possessions, the servants, and the power, whose father had been killed in a celebrated accident, which was followed by the death of her second husband and the expiry of her third between the thighs of a deranged woman, and of whose first husband no information has until now become available.[4] Madame Fawqiya had not become disheartened, but had opened her luxurious house at night to people of standing, excellence, and eminence, there to quaff draughts of scholarship, conversation, ease, food, and literature and to discuss such topics as al-Na'isa, Diyab, Abu Nuwas, the Constitution, the British, Imam al-Shafi'i, Makram Ebeid, and Najib al-Rihani.

It is believed that Umm Nu'man experienced a tangible thrill on accompanying her only son to surrender him to the distinguished lady in the hope that she would purchase him. She washed his body with half the water in the Bahr Yusuf, dressed him in all his jallabiyas, and made a detour to take him to the house of Eid the Barber, who cropped his head leaving only the tuft of hair at the front of his naked pate, a tuft which was not to be cut until a kid had been slaughtered, in fulfillment of a vow made to Sheikh al-Farghal. Then she stuffed his pockets with dates and ta'miya—a rite of farewell she felt to be indispensable—kissed him numerous times, and set off with him for the lady's house, where they arrived in the evening.

Eventually, Umm Nu'man found herself, with her son, before the lady. However, she did not find herself there directly. Indeed, she stood, and then sat, for a long time at the threshold of the salon, which was lit by four incandescent lamps, while Madame Fawqiya, with her beaming face and soft, full body, listened with absorption to the issues being discussed by the village's learned-as-an-ocean jurisprudent, Sheikh Ali, and Sheikh Abu Tis'a. The first was arguing with the second, for the one hundred thousandth time, over the significance of the sobriquet 'Abu Tis'a' ('He of the Nines') that was applied to him, and Abu Tis'a, for the millionth time, was saying that his father had regarded it as auspicious that God, Almighty and Glorious, had shown such concern for that number, for among the Almighty's Miraculous and Pure Verses were to be found:

1. *We gave Moses nine clear signs.* (Surat al-Isra')
2. *And they tarried in the Cave three hundred years, and to that they added nine more.* (Surat al-Kahf)
3. *It scorches the flesh of humans; there are nineteen in charge of it.* (Surat al-Muddathir)
4. *Behold, this my brother has ninety-nine ewes and I have one ewe.* (Surat Sad)

To this, Sheikh Abu Tis'a added that his father had had nine boy children and nine girls, that he himself had fathered seven, and that he prayed to God to extend His blessings so far as to allow him to follow the example of His Miraculous Verses and father nine, or, if He were not feeling stingy, nineteen, or even, were He feeling expansive, ninety-nine.

At this, Sheikh Ali cried out in challenge to Sheikh Abu Tis'a, "If that is the case, O Sheikh of the Devils, why do you flee God's words in Surat al-Naml?" at which Madame Fawqiya asked delightedly, for the millionth time, "And what does it say in Surat al-Naml, Sheikh Ali?" and Sheikh Ali stood up (the seat pad of the chair falling as a result between his feet) and recited, "*There were nine men in the city who spread corruption in the land!*"

At this exquisite moment, when the audience had been won over to Sheikh Ali's side and were displaying their unbounded admiration for his cleverness, Madame Fawqiya caught sight of Nu'man and his mother in the entrance to the salon and beckoned them into her presence.

We will not dispute the events that followed: Madame Fawqiya extended her hand, which Umm Nu'man kissed, and she extended her hand to the boy Nu'man, who did not kiss it despite his mother's digs in his ribs and his back. This made Madame Fawqiya laugh in magnificent humility, and she rubbed the discomfited Nu'man's head with her delicate hand, then passed her fingertips around his nape and ears and came back to his head and touched his topknot, the assembled notables, out of respect, maintaining silence. She asked Nu'man his name but he did not reply, so the lady laughed and asked him again, and Umm Nu'man answered her. Madame Fawqiya now asked Umm Nu'man to take her ease, so she withdrew backward and returned to sit down on the floor of the salon entrance.

Nu'man surrendered himself to the mounting stupor in his ears and head from the lights of the incandescent lamps and Madame Fawqiya's fingertips. She indicated to him that he should sit down near her, so he drew into himself even further and shrank down next to her left leg, while conversation continued among the assembled persons on the following topics:

  a. The reasons for the murder of Musa Aqladiyus and the throwing of his body into the monastery canal.
  b. The reason for the delay in the conversion to Islam of Umar ibn al-Khattab.

c. The story of a nun at the Mistress of Apostles school who had sinned with a rich girl student.

d. The outcome of the investigations in the Fakhri murder case.

e. The belief that Amin Abu Illa was hiding his top-quality aragi and only sending them Asyuti aragi or regular raisin-liquor, and the need for a reevaluation of their relationship with him.

f. The likelihood of being able to get rid of the doctor at the community clinic, whose name was associated with certain dubious practices.

g. The peace treaty of al-Hudaybiya.

h. The she-camel that had given birth to a cockerel in a nearby village.

i. The rise in the cost of straw, red brick, and timber.

j. Extensive and impolite discourse on the subject of Abu Nuwas and the slave girl Jinan.

k. The tale of how a ruler of olden times had been castrated at the hands of his slaves.

Down on the ground, Nu'man had lost his concentration and was no longer capable of following the movements of lips, necks, and eyes; had the men not been making merry with such loud voices, sparkling glasses in hand, he would have dropped off. His mother was still sitting cross-legged in the entrance, dazzled and overjoyed and calling down on those assembled prayers for their welfare and good fortune, when Hamdi the Poultryman made a sign to Nu'man. When the boy failed to understand the sign, the man hurried over to him, picked him up, and lifted him till Nu'man's face touched the flame of one of the lamps. Everyone laughed, but Hamdi the Poultryman threw the little boy toward Sheikh Ahmad

Muhammadayn, the sugar refinery broker, who stood up and quickly snatched the body from the air, regardless of Umm Nu'man's scream of terror. Everyone in the salon formed a circle, and Nu'man became a body flying through the air that scarcely had time to come to rest in the arms of one man before it was thrown into another's, while their bodies, flown with food and chatter, flushed with geniality and good cheer, exerted themselves to have Nu'man provide pleasure for them in those rare moments as he flew through the air of the salon only to be snatched up by tender hands and fastened on by mustached mouths while the noble lady laughed and laughed till the tears ran from her compassionate eyes. Umm Nu'man's screams, stifled or not, did nothing but increase the enjoyment ("What are you afraid of, crazy woman?"), as the ceiling swooped and receded, the fiery blast of the lamps retreated and approached, and Nu'man's body was shaken almost to bits, despite which the happy uproar continued in the enjoyment of these mighty pendulations, and ribald talk erupted through the air of the tumultuous salon, creating a magic circle of extravagant pleasure. In the end, Madame Fawqiya was moved to request everyone to desist, but no one could hear and the laughter, comments, and tossings continued unabated until Sheikh Ali the Poultryman grew exhausted, followed by Mahmud, clerk of the market, then by another Mahmud, clerk of the slaughterhouse, followed by Abu Tis'a, followed by Sheikh Ahmad, the school principal,[5] followed by a third Mahmud, clerk of the community center, followed by Sheikh Rashid (who was blind), followed by the other Ahmad, broker of the sugar refinery, who all became exhausted and rushed to their seats releasing their last laughs, remaining comments, and a general diffusion of merriment and happiness. No one was left moving in the salon but three—Madame Fawqiya, who could not hide her merry, happy excitement, Nuʿman, who could not hide his weeping, tearful excitement, and Umm Nuʿman, who could not hide her weak, ineffectual excitement, which made its way into her very tears as she stretched out her arms to her son, sobbing, "If only your father had been alive, my child . . . !"

She did not continue, for Umm Nuʿman was unaware that what she had, unknowingly, said at that moment was in line with the calumny of that slanderer who has accused me of colluding in the premature removal of Abu Nuʿman and so including Nuʿman in the list of prodigy-performing and miracle-working orphans. It saddens me to have to report that Umm Nuʿman departed for her hut in the open spaces, leaving Nuʿman standing before Madame Fawqiya, whose beautiful fingertips caressed the forelock that was dedicated to Sheikh al-Farghal and could be removed only after the slaughter of a kid. Quiet returned to the salon and people started to discuss the reasons for al-ʿAqqad's[6] turning against the Wafd and a bout of happy belching, perfumed with the last vestiges of their merriment, set upon them. Nuʿman was silent and calm, slumped between the lady's legs. Mahmud al-ʿIsawi, a few hours previously, had encountered Ahmad Mahir Basha in the pharaonic hall that separates the House of Representatives from the Senate and opened fire on the prime minister, causing him to fall, soaked in blood, a few minutes before his intended proclamation of war against the Axis countries. Some hours later, Madame Fawqiya ordered Nuʿman Abd al-Hafiz Khamis to be carried to her upper-floor quarters, the majestic lady having conceived the desire to bestow a further token of mercy and affection on his noble body.

---

1. This opinion of our friend of the fleeting intelligence derives from the experience he gained from the job that he formerly practiced

in a government department with secret expenditures. Our friend resigned and returned to his place of birth, where he purchased a house, a wife with her children, seven faddans, and half a canal.

2. The first signs of the flood appear immediately following the wheat harvest and are themselves followed by the ripening of the dates, the spread of mange among the camels, a readiness to engage in the making of groats, the storing of straw, the manufacture of pots, the appearance of mendicant dill-sellers, and the leaping of the male farm animals onto the female.

3. A kind of cured salted fish, the largest so treated.

4. It is reported that the noble lady's first husband was struck dumb by devils at the moment of his discovery of certain scandalous goings-on in his house and that he dwells to this day in reclusion, on his own, having intercourse with none. Another report has it that he was murdered by the hand of the third husband, and there are further reports in circulation to the effect that he roams the lands of God wearing sackcloth. All of these claims are, however, without substantiation.

5. Sheikh Ahmad the school principal was a relative of Nu'man's and we will likely devote a separate chapter to him.

6. Abbas Mahmud al-'Aqqad (1889–1964), one of the great Egyptian intellectuals of the first sixty years of the twentieth century. He never married and worked for a time (up to 1935) as a Wafd Party activist and defender of its causes. Thereafter he turned against the Wafd and remained antagonistic toward it for no clear reason.

For the Majestic, and Also Beautiful, Lady!

T he majestic, and also beautiful, lady who had decided to acquire Nu'man Abd al-Hafiz for her magnificent house was composed of a nose, two lips, two eyes, two eyebrows, two cheeks, and a neck, followed by a chest, two breasts, a navel, and two thighs, which were components rarely found gathered together, and complete, in the women of our village, whose particulars hung loosely by reason of the constant changes in the climate and such factors as erosion, heat, children, mud, dung, cold, and men.

It is believed that certain individuals—a very few—have suffered violent ends on their discovery of the differences between the components of the majestic lady's body and those of other women. Naturally, I am not referring to stories Jayyid Abd al-Nur gave rise to when he hid among them from the eyes of the British in the twenties,[1] nor the tales told by Sa'id the Black, the friend of Father Abd al-Guddus, the monk at the famous Muharraq Monastery,[2] nor the reports concerning a trader in molasses who was found murdered in the wake of the demise of the majestic lady's second husband, since all of these may be exaggerated—even if everyone agrees that the majestic lady was wont to loll about in a bath of milk, sleep naked on her belly under the sun of Bashans, take her life in her hands by visiting graveyards in the dark, and dance wildly to the music of a senile gypsy spike-fiddle player afflicted by an unknown disease in the lower half of his body who resided for a period among her servants.

It was, however, the combination of all these things that provided us, during the years of alteration and transformation, unveiling and revealing, with that amazing human body that was capable of bounty, the fingertips of which were extended to fondle the forelock that was dedicated to Sheikh al-Farghal and which could be removed only after the slaughter of a kid.

It may be that we shall require a great deal of painstaking research to become fully apprised of what took place between our majestic, and also beautiful, lady and Nu'man Abd al-Hafiz Khamis on that night on which the conversation began with al-'Aqqad's attack on the Wafd and ended with the reveling notables tossing Nu'man's body back and forth out of high spirits, nocturnal conviviality, and intoxication.

Furthermore, and while excluding the version of events reported by the late Sheikh Thabit Abd al-Rahman (whose intention was to sow uncertainty as to what happened), and overlooking the account given by Sheikh Rashid on this matter, and given our slowly dawning comprehension, reached in spite of the inadequate knowledge of the informants, whom the majestic lady had left in the salon resolved to make their departure at the end of the night, and given our focused and intense insistence on removing any obscurity confronting the life of Nu'man, we find ourselves obliged to deal forthrightly with the incident, with neither fear nor dread.

Nu'man himself, despite his apprehension and alarm, felt a tranquilizing peace of mind steal warmly via the majestic lady's hand into his clean- (but for the forelock) shaven pate. On the stairs, made of marble imported from the lands of alabaster in the days when the majestic lady's father was a Wafdist deputy in the House of Representatives, Nu'man nearly balked, and for the first time since the moment of the lady's decision to acquire him, he came to a stop, on the twentieth step, but the lady laughed and once again placed her hand on Nu'man's head. On the twenty-fifth step, on which, it is said, the majestic lady's father had been murdered some years previously, Nu'man came to a stop for the second time, but the lady's joy only increased and she urged him to be happy, though Nu'man felt that the world had grown smaller and became aware of the absence from it of acacia trees, the waters of the Bahr Yusuf, the twistings of the roads and the river banks, and the curvings of the canals; the hand of the majestic lady, however, left his shaven head and descended a quarter of a hand's breadth to Nu'man's neck, thus exerting a certain pressure to the propulsion of the boy's body. This made Nu'man shiver and balk the more, and a feeling of loneliness breached him, and he missed his mother; indeed, he even missed his father (and he an orphan!). However, a majestic lady was pressing on his neck to make him climb the ten remaining stairs and the boy yielded and stepped out, and the lady grew merrier yet.

Inside the majestic lady's quarters, Nu'man stood still. Intricate works of wood, gilded frames containing pictures of men wearing medals and mustaches, a floor spread with colored wool. No trace of earthenware vessels, braziers, chintz garments, cans of salted fish, or rush mats. Everything was ornamented in blood red, desert yellow, plant green, and sky blue. The majestic lady continued to move on through the apartments, calling on Nu'man to precede her, and with every step Nu'man took, the lady would laugh and extend her hand in an attempt to calm the boy's skittishness.

The lady opened a door, went through it, and returned. She made a turn around the apartments, opened another door, went through it, and returned and stood in front of Nu'man, whom she lifted up in front of her and stood on a sofa, gazing long into his face. The boy became flustered, but a moment of calm flooded over him and he decided to hold fast. Indeed, his foxy eyes started to widen and allow the whole scene to penetrate his innermost being.

When the lady extended her hands to Nu'man he responded to her and stretched out his own, and the lady would have started laughing once more had not Nu'man drawn himself to his full boyish height, his feet burying themselves in the flower-embroidered mattress of the sofa, at which point the lady stretched her hand out to Nu'man's face, while his eyes turned aside, to the glowing incandescent lamp that hissed with the hiss of his estrangement from home, the strangeness of everything around him, and his own feeling that he was a stranger. The lady started roaming the apartments once more, passing through doors and returning to Nu'man, but soon pulled gently on Nu'man's hand and drew him toward the bathroom.

The bathroom of the majestic, and also beautiful, lady had been designed by an Italian monk who was said to have memorized the Noble Qur'an,[3] and this was apparent from the angles where the ornamental elements of the bathroom corners met the ceiling, arcs of a purple hue joining there with others of a delicate violet color to form semicircles that meshed until they touched the panes of glass of the upper windows. Parts of the right-hand wall had fallen and two glass panes had cracked the day of the first mishap, in which the majestic lady's third husband had been stabbed in the shoulder with a lance. Subsequently, the middle door had come off its hinges, and the glass opposite had been smashed the night certain guests had exceeded the bounds of proper decorum and tossed the seats around and fought one another with their drinking glasses. No further dangerous consequences had arisen, with the exception of the breaking of the skull of Abd Rabbih, who had spent some time as a servant to the mistress of the house.

When Nu'man's feet touched the bathroom tiles, he felt a gentle thrill pass through the coarse skin and move on to the marrow faster than bilharzia, but the lady continued to be intoxicated with pleasure at everything that Nu'man experienced. Her fingertips left the boy's topknot only to return to his neck, and Nu'man, feeling that things were safe, started to obey her, at ease with her fingers. She then reached for Nu'man's jallabiya and stripped it off him, laughing, to reveal the small grey body, covered in bruises made by trees, holes, and rocks, which the majestic, and also beautiful, lady's smile embraced as a feather-lined nest does the raven's chick. She had not believed, up to that moment, that Nu'man wore his jallabiya next to the skin. What was amusing was that Nu'man raced after his jallabiya in an attempt to recover it, which made the majestic lady laugh once more. However, he forgot all about the jallabiya, which he was afraid of losing, the moment a cascade of water, spurting from the roof, accosted him. Nu'man was terrified, or screamed. The majestic lady laughed, or said nothing. What mattered was that the water—coming from some place that had no relation to the Bahr Yusuf—poured down over Nu'man. How delicious was the pleasure on the body and the shaven head with its nodding topknot as Nu'man revived amid the bubbles of white soap whose smell was sweeter even than that of gurilla flowers![4]

For the first time in his life, Nu'man stepped out of water into a bath towel like velvet that so enswathed him as almost to cause him to fall asleep in its folds. When the lady returned to him, he was standing in the middle of the apartment feasting his eyes on his naked body reflected on the surface of the huge mirror, the towel fallen at his cracked feet. The majestic lady, however, had disburdened herself of some of her garments, leaving only a shift diaphanous as clear water, her white body undulating like the moon when submerged in the shallow depths of the waters at the foot of the hut of reeds; full and white, at ease beneath its shift, was the majestic lady's body. Then she clapped her hands, laughing, and asked Nu'man to tell her something.

Needless to say, Nu'man did not relate anything concerning the murder of Ahmad Mahir Basha in the pharaonic hall that separates the House of Representatives from the Senate as he was on his way to proclaim war against Adolph Hitler and others. Similarly, he said nothing of how Salim the Ruined had his store closed, or the incident in which Hajj Zahir had shaved off the mustache of one of the giants of the North Side after throwing him to the ground and standing atop his body in the street, or the rumor that had gone round the village of Sheikh Ahmad Abd al-Majid's intention to divest himself of turban and caftan in favor of jacket and tarbush to prepare the way for his marriage to a woman from Cairo, or even the woman who had consorted with an ape in the graveyard. What Nu'man did tell—or so it is believed—and that with helpful interventions from the lady herself, was something about stealing taro, and setting fires in the sugarcane, and a detailed description of a fox's or a jackal's eyes, and how Umm Nu'man's leg had swelled up, and how a boat had sunk in the Bahr Yusuf, and the longest catfish he'd ever seen in his life.

The majestic lady remained intoxicated, circling around Nuʿman and encouraging him lovingly until both of them fell silent.

Till this day we have not got to the bottom of what it was exactly that the majestic lady set turning in her apartment, producing a heart-rending music. Some say it was a song-machine, others a broadcasting instrument. Some say it was one of those magic potions that Father Abd al-Guddus had left at her house during his repeated attempts to provide the majestic lady with the opportunity to bear children. What is sure is that the music welled forth, sending ecstasy through the whole apartment till the boy's body shook. Soon, the majestic lady had joined in the rhythm with a sweet clapping and was pulling Nuʿman to the middle of the velvety space, her wide, soulful eyes closing and opening in happy wakefulness. And soon Nuʿman had fallen under the spell of the beguiling magic, raising his arms and bending his naked waist, as the lady circled around him, lips pressed together.

It is no longer possible to monitor everything that happened thereafter. Some speak of the dancing reaching a climax at which the majestic lady removed her diaphanous garment and took Nuʿman to her bosom, melting into his body so that the sweat flowed around them causing the lamplight to refract. Some speak of the majestic lady's weeping convulsively as she knelt before Nuʿman's body and rolled her head against the soles of his feet. Some speak of savage, lustful kisses covering every inch of the boy's body. Some speak of annihilating, tumultuous, unbridled passion. Some speak of quiet moments in which the majestic lady clasped Nuʿman's body to her and settled him atop her thighs, inviting him to sleep.

The only person who could help us to throw light on the matter is Nuʿman himself, but Nuʿman—or so Sheikh Thabit

Abd al-Rahman charges—was afflicted with the same sickness of reticence that led to the death of his father, Abd al-Hafiz Khamis, and which is the same disease that has draped the life of certain virtuous persons with shame, for they could not arrive at any way to harmonize what happened with the painful image that the boy presented to them as he ran, at the end of that night, naked and screaming through the lanes of the village, the dogs barking after him and the people peeping from behind the doors of dawn, refusing to acknowledge what had happened, which was that Nu'man had traversed the entire village till he reached the first acacia tree at the edge of the dyke, where, when his feet touched the thorns of the bank, he felt the shudder of the return to absolute liberty, a liberty that brought Nu'man back to the solid ground of his life—after which he lost no time in resting his head against the trunk of the tree, his limbs relaxing as he listened to the chirruping of the crickets.

---

1. Jayyid Abd al-Nur was a hero of the attack on the British train at Dayrut in 1919, having snatched a pair of binoculars out of the hand of the wife of Bob, the commanding officer, at the moment the latter was being killed. He lived for a long time as a fugitive from the British, hiding in people's houses. Then, in the fifties, he emerged, destitute and ragged, and tried to make a living raising pigs, but failed. He died in 1957.

2. Father Abd al-Guddus, who was killed two years ago riding his donkey on the Biblaw road, was the Upper Egyptian equivalent of Russia's Rasputin. He dealt in magic and legerdemain, and this endowed him with an astonishing degree of influence over the women of the wealthy classes in Upper Egypt. It is said that he lived to an age of one hundred and twenty.

3. The Italian monk was invited to the house of the majestic lady's father following the peace council that was convened between the Mu'awwad and Gummus families at which a settlement of their conflict was reached that led to the demise of numerous people not one of whom belonged to either.

4. *Gurilla:* a plant of the lily family that grows abundantly in the fields of central Upper Egypt among the clover and wheat. The flowers are yellow, it is sweet-smelling, and some villagers eat it.

An Intermediate Chapter

o be even-handed, I have to declare my reservations
about accepting the disturbing statement made by a
certain scoundrel against the Khamis lineage, among
whom Nuʻman is to be numbered, to the effect, apparently,
that they are a people lacking in discernment: when they
come across a purse full of gold, they undo the cloth purse,
filch it, and leave the gold,[1] and if one of them in those days
had recourse to a moneylender to buy a sack of chemical
fertilizer, he would pay the price of it many times over, and
in installments, and sell the sack immediately for half its real
value in order to buy tea and tobacco. This undeniably means
no more than that they were individuals to whom had not
been granted the same opportunities for refinement that Abd
al-ʻAl Hifnawi made possible for their paternal cousins.[2]

It is regrettable that we should be forced to have recourse
to this type of thing to defend Nuʻman against this scoundrel's
disturbing accusation of heartlessness while at the same time
refusing to take sides against him with his mother in the
immediate aftermath of the events described in the preceding
chapter, at the end of which he returned from the majestic,
and also beautiful, lady's palace naked and dismayed.

There can be no doubt at all that a question mark will hang for ever over Umm Nu'man for the harsh repudiation with which she confronted her only son as he stood at dawn, in a state of collapse, at the door of her hut. She repudiated him with the harshness of Ibn Abi Sufyan rejecting the messenger of Ibn Abi Talib when he came from Medina to demand the Commander of Syria's allegiance,[3] and she insisted on announcing to whatever fields might hear her, in clear and burning tones, that she had suffered catastrophe twice in her life—the first time when she had married Abd al-Hafiz Khamis, and the second when she had born him a child—overlooking the fact that Nu'man, who was standing at the entrance to the hut and shivering, was, equally, standing on the threshold of adolescence, that stage of life to which Sigmund Freud attributes such immeasurable importance.

That autumn dawn, the fields witnessed a painful exchange between Umm Nu'man, who had wished to introduce her only son into the circle of the majestic lady's entourage so that he might strut in the glory of the incandescent lamps, the meats, the rice, the tea, and the potatoes, and her son, the destroyer of her dreams, that idiotic boy who had insisted on leaving the gold while not even filching the purse. In the end, Umm Nu'man—she over whom a question mark will forever hang—could find nothing else to do than to smack the face of the bastard son of a bastard with a hefty lump of mud.

Nu'man set off for he knew not where. He abandoned the hut and did not return to the village. He wandered among the fields, under the sycamore figs and among the camel thorn, esparto grass, and cattail wastes, carrying his topknot on the crown of his shaven head and inside it the upsetting and exciting ghosts of his night with the majestic lady, beset by the same pleasurable thrills that he felt whenever he jumped into the water, or climbed a tree trunk, or pulled a cow's tail and yet remaining, eternally, himself, Nu'man Abd al-Hafiz Khamis, who brought the matter to a close by putting an arm beneath his head in the shadow of some pile or other of reeds and going to sleep.

Nu'man Abd al-Hafiz was never wicked. He never attempted to test his ability to stare into the eye of the sun. If anyone asked him, "Where are you off to, Nu'man?" he would put his hand over his eyes and tilt his head backward to avoid looking at his questioner, who, before Nu'man had time to answer, would request his assistance in pulling the donkey while it stepped over a hole or a ditch, or dragging an animal to market, or following along after a young donkey that was carrying manure, or shucking corn cobs, or shooing a cow to keep it going round with the waterwheel, or making a she-camel kneel, or loosening the tether of a she-buffalo that was refusing the advances of a youth in heat, or buying supplies and cigarettes for the day-laborers at their work, or answering the inquiries of field thieves. And even if you weren't looking for Nu'man, you would find him there in front of you, in the meadow or west of the bridge, at Hawwash or al-Tawil, at al-Kalbi or al-Hisa'i, leaving the mighty village to busy itself with its own affairs, such as the killing of Yanni the baker, and Aziz Effendi's wife, and Ali Abd al-Nazir, and Hasan al-Banna, and Sanyura, and al-Nuqrashi, and Fanus, and Abd al-Qadir Taha, and Hasab al-Nabi, not to mention the burning of the wheat and sugarcane fields, the flooding of the fava beans, the tearing to pieces of the body of Uncle Rizq's only son,[4] the expanding of three wings of its houses of ill repute, for pleasure and enjoyment, and the supporting of, on one occasion, the Constitutional Liberals and, on another, the Wafd, thus increasing the number of those killed. Meanwhile, Sheikh al-Shinnawi continued to distribute inheritance shares, destruction, and trickery in the houses of the village according to the scales of justice, while Umm Nuʿman sat in her hut lamenting her unhappy lot and Nuʿman ran around in the fields carrying provisions, shooing animals, and dragging behind him the shrieking memories of his night with the majestic lady. From time to time, he would permit himself to stretch out his fingers and touch the thigh of a woman in a cotton shed, or jump behind a girl on the back of a jenny to prevent the girl from falling off the dyke, or allow his body to rub up against that of a woman as he helped her to raise a jar of water, or inadvertently fail to close his eyes when one of them bent over to collect fallen ears of wheat. Never, however, if the truth be told, was he like that Diyab who was mentioned in a novel that appeared in the fifties, the one who couldn't keep his hands off the animals.[5]

It appears to me that the real danger that prevents us from settling down is that the Lord opened things with us as fishermen, or shepherds, and ended them after we'd been lured into becoming peasants. A greater degree of acumen was called for if we were to understand how the game should then be played. In ancient times, the mountains penned us in, so we set off for the shores, the cattail forests, the acacia stands, and the thickets of palm trees and houses, paying no attention to the fact that all that was left to us out of the whole business was a collection of prohibitions, warnings, and commandments, starting with "Thou shalt not steal" and ending up with "Early to bed, early to rise," it being noted along the way that one should not put off till tomorrow what one could do today, forget the rights of neighbors, commit adultery, talk about people behind their backs, or attack the reputations of decent ladies, and that one should pray and give alms, and all that sort of thing.

Nu'man, however, didn't care. He threw all the achievements of history behind him and kept on going, roaming in the fields, leading the cotton-picking gangs, harvesting the wheat, pounding the corn, slipping into mosques, weddings, funerals, Sufi ceremonies, and ghawazee performances, till one day he awoke to the fact that his feet were leading him to Isma'il the Gravedigger.

The gravedigger—Isma'il—was a taciturn type. He had committed to memory the dimensions of all the bodies, and body parts, that our village had buried since the day Our Master Yusuf dug his famous canal, the Bahr Yusuf. Should the South Side turn on the North Side, Isma'il the Gravedigger would be standing at the entrance to the tombs, waiting. When bullets and screams rang out and fires burned, he just kept lighting cigarettes, his gaze seemingly preoccupied with something in the sky, and at the end of the day, or the following morning at the latest, the first arrivals would appear, wrapped in shrouds and borne on men's shoulders, the hymn of supplication from al-Busiri's *Mantle* sounding behind them.

When Nu'man's shadow fell across Isma'il's face as he lay on the dirt that edged the last of the graves, blocking the sun, and when the gravedigger moved to welcome Nu'man, the weather was summery, and the gravedigger smiled slowly. Then he straightened up and indicated to Nu'man that he should sit, and the boy felt a sense of ease.

On the first day, Nu'man helped Isma'il the Gravedigger sprinkle water in front of the tombs of certain notables whose heirs took care for their comfort. On the second day, he watered the cactuses of people of high social status. On the sixth day, he participated in the opening of the entrance to a grave. On the tenth day, Isma'il lowered him from the top aperture of a recently used tomb to strip off a few shrouds.

On the hundredth day, Isma'il the Gravedigger took Nu'man by the hand and spent some time roaming with him among the tombs and explaining the reasons behind the growing number of residents in each. He finished by bringing him to a halt in front of a tomb whose doors were off their hinges and on which were drawn horses, steamboats, airplanes, and a camel. Nu'man stayed unmoving in front of the tomb so long that the gravedigger shook him and said, laughing, "You can spend the night here, my boy."

Nu'man was overcome by a wave of emotion, followed by a sense of security, surrender, and peace, and he decided to go home and visit his mother.

---

1. Sheikh Thabit Abd al-Rahman is the one believed to have described the Khamis clan as heartless. Though it is said that Sheikh Thabit described the Khamis clan thus, experience proves that this characteristic can, without misgiving, be attributed to other families.

2. Abd al-'Al Hifnawi's brothers lived under his protection and left to him alone the management of their land and real estate. He then proceeded to marry his daughters to individuals from families other than his own, and outsiders inherited all the real estate and land, leaving the family of the original testator to survive from hand to mouth.

3. Even if we are to suppose that Umm Nu'man acted in this way, the comparison would contain an important error, since Ali Ibn Abi Talib sent to Mu'awiya in Syria one of the companions of the Prophet (blessings and peace be upon him), namely Jarir Ibn Abd Allah al-Bajli, to ask him to enter into the same compact as the rest of the people, which is to say, to declare their allegiance to Ibn Abi Talib as Commander of the Faithful, citing such reasons and proofs as the latter's kinship with the Prophet (blessings and peace be upon him), the early date of his conversion to Islam, his sacrifices, struggle, and migration from Mecca to Medina, these being attributes of which Mu'awiya and his son were innocent. However, Mu'awiya listened to the ambassador and said nothing, instead putting him off and continuing to do so at great length, while at the same time summoning the leading men of Syria and

the heads of the army as though to consult their opinions of Ali's request, but continually making an issue of the murder of Uthman (the previous Commander of the Faithful) and urging them to remain faithful to the murdered caliph and seek revenge for his death. Mu'awiya was certainly too wise to expose himself to accusations of harshness or injury to, or mistreatment of, the ambassadors who were sent. See on this matter Part Two of *The Great Strife (al-Fitna al-kubra)* by Dr. Taha Hussein. It seems likely that this comparison was foisted on the writer by the religious.

4. A certain notable kidnapped Uncle Rizq's young son, whom God had blessed him with after five daughters, and confined him in a sugarcane field till such time as the ransom should be paid. Uncle Rizq sold a camel, a cow, and copper pots, in full sight and hearing of the village, to ransom his son, and after the money was paid it was discovered that he had been killed by a wild animal.

5. Diyab is the son of Ahmad Effendi in the novel *The Land* written by Abd al-Rahman al-Sharqawi. He is greedy and unsophisticated, loves ta'miya, and practices abominations with animals. His behavior was received with revulsion in central Upper Egypt.

On the Empty Tomb

*A*ny historian is bound to be afflicted by panic and confusion when he discovers that his hero—the vehicle of his theory—is hiding from him matters of the utmost sensitivity, matters whose revelation may have repercussions on the challenge and response that—so we are told—govern the progress of history, matters that may even subject the entire theory to collapse.

We have gone the length of the preceding chapters believing that the topknot of hair crowning Nu'man's pate was nothing but a freely growing 'ex-voto' dedicated to Sheikh al-Farghal that could be shaved off only once a kid had been slaughtered at the threshold to his tomb, and everything that happened has served to reinforce this narrow perception. Umm Nu'man, in her hut, buried her pain deep beneath her never-ending struggle, near the banks of the Bahr Yusuf, to augment her trade in salted fish and summer dates with certain medicinal products, such as chicory and cassia seed; the majestic, and also beautiful, lady said nothing to anyone, friend or stranger, of anything that may have caught her attention during her wanton night with Nu'man; the barbers, from Hajj Yasin and Eid to Abd al-Latif and Musa, alerted no one to the relationship between the topknot ex-voto and any other occurrence; and Nu'man passed from season to season, went through fields and experiences, canals and houses, jumped into ditches, fished, and climbed trees without, the scoundrel, alerting us to what that topknot meant until he, Nu'man, grew up, the tip of his nose developed, his voice broke, his muscles hardened, and his mustache sprouted, while the sheikhs of the village—its lords and masters—passed the time in talk of Kamil Tamir, Shawqi Tamir, Sam'an al-Gummus, the war in Palestine, Anwar Musa, Sheikh al-Sabbagh, dancing girls, and Anwar Sharif's radio, leaving Nu'man in the company of Isma'il the digger—or delver—of graves, so that we find Nu'man in the end quite simply taking up residence in a tomb of unknown ownership with an exceedingly elegant superstructure whose walls were tattooed with ships, horses, airplanes, steamboats, and a camel (a camel whose roar you could hear seven graveyards away).

The sad thing is that we were on the point of going along with Nu'man in this life of his among the shrouds, sorrows, and dirges, and we would have done so, had not fate brought us a woman from a neighboring settlement whom the fanatical adherents of the demons had sentenced, as treatment for a swelling in her buttocks and a redness where her thighs met, to bury herself at dawn in the sands of an abandoned tomb and then, at sunrise, sprinkle herself with salt water ninety-nine times.

Isma'il the Gravedigger knew this woman well and had probably taken payment from her to direct her to the place where she might be cured. She arrived in the late afternoon of a day in the third week of the month of Abib of the Coptic year 1668, bearing under her arm a cloth purse, a jackknife, and an earthenware vessel, and the gravedigger led her through the lanes of al-Bughayli (the official name of the area where the dead were buried) till he brought her to the abandoned tomb, in front of which sat Nu'man, plaiting a palm-fiber rope.

At first, Nu'man felt dread of the woman with the downcast looks. He thought she was looking for the grave of some dear departed and wanted to perform her obligation to pray for mercy on his soul. Then he thought that she must be some woman from the villages who had lost her way. Then he thought she must be a gypsy woman come in from the desert to buy dead men's ribs over which to make spells.

When the gravedigger Isma'il made it clear to him who the woman was, Nu'man felt even greater dread, for he remembered how, a few days before, he had tried to visit his mother but had been prevented from carrying out his mission by the fighting that had broken out between the North and South sides and the resulting closure of the roads to travelers. Nu'man therefore tried to escape, but Isma'il the Gravedigger turned his back, throwing out his final instruction: "Prepare the square!"

The rules for therapeutic burial stipulate the following:

1. The (equal-sided) square must be marked out on smooth sand containing neither pebbles, lime, nor refuse, with markers made of branches from male palm trees with no fronds removed. (In case of the treatment of young girls, the rules stipulate that the branches must be from male palm trees with white fronds, which is to say, from the heart of the palm.)

2. The chapter of the Qur'an known as *The Everlasting Refuge* plus two verses from *Iron* and two from *Repentance* are to be recited over each branch.

3. The square is to be sprinkled with water and left until it has dried.

4. The patient is to dig the hole himself, bearing in mind that the orientation of the head is to be:
    a. On moonlit nights:
        i. south facing for men and old women;
        ii. south facing with a slight turn to the east for young men and widows;
    b. On dark nights:
        i. unimportant, as the demons will make adjustments to the placement in such a way as to benefit the treatment.

5. Digging of the hole must never begin after sunset, and the marking of the square with palm branches must never be done before sunset.

6. Dry palm branches, or those with fronds removed, must not be used.

7. The burial must begin at midnight, and no unbeliever, polytheist, or person with the letter *shin* in his name, or who has been charged with adultery or lost male children or not been circumcised, may take part in the filling of the hole with sand.

Isma'il the Gravedigger brought Nu'man the palm branches just as he finished the preparation of the square, the woman sitting the while on her backside in a corner of the tomb uttering prayers for their safety and well-being. The two of them observed precisely all the rules for treatment current in the area, notwithstanding slight differences in other localities as to orientation, the method for filling in the sand, and the linking of the beginning of the interment in the sand to the appearance in the sky of the Ursae, Major and Minor.

Next, Isma'il the Gravedigger gave the woman permission to start preparing her burial, and she extended her hands into the center of the circle and, stepping over the palm fronds, started raising the sand in her cupped palms until she had piled it next to the walls of the tomb. When she grew tired, she took off her black jallabiya and fashioned from it something for moving the sand. Dark enshrouded the tomb, and Nu'man and Isma'il sat at the door, unmoving.

We do not know why the woman wept when she had finished preparing the hole, for it was in keeping with the prescriptions, and Isma'il the Gravedigger praised her when he began probing its depths and looking for faults. Isma'il the Gravedigger then pronounced the hole suitable for therapy and asked the wailing woman to remove the rest of her clothes. She arose, embarrassed, the darkness of the tomb covering her movements—though the darkness didn't matter, the treatment being more important than the darkness—and if this was the first experience of such things for Nu'man, it was the thousandth for Isma'il the Gravedigger, which is why he proceeded toward the woman, raised her arms in the air, stripped her of her two jallabiyas and her drawers, and ordered her to stop sobbing.

Everything was clear in the dark. Sickly reflections of starlight infiltrated, surrounding their bodies with pale, delicate outlines. Isma'il the Gravedigger's hand reached out to the woman's torso as he asked God to make of it a blessed step and beseeched Heaven to rid her of disease. Nu'man's arm reached out to the naked woman's hand in confusion and he shivered, causing Isma'il the Gravedigger to yell at him. The woman made a mistake by moving her left foot forward, so he made her go back and start the motion with her right foot. The gray night cast its feeble light over the ghostly shapes of the place, and the silence of the other world enveloped this.

When the initial procedures had been correctly performed, and the woman had succeeded in reaching the beginning of the hole, the gravedigger bent her over backward so that she was supporting herself on Nu'man's arm, and her legs began to slip into the depths. A portion of the chapter *Yasin* flowed from the gravedigger's mouth, for this creates high walls of protection, hope, proximity to angels, and expulsion of devils, and eventually the woman settled comfortably into the hole; all that was left outside was her sad, agitated, trembling head. At this point, the gravedigger asked Nu'man to begin pouring the dirt down onto the ulcerated body.

With care and persistence, Nu'man buried the woman. He brought the sand in the jallabiya that the woman had taken off and he packed it around her legs. The gravedigger ordered him to recite something, but Nu'man excused himself on the grounds that he didn't know it, so the gravedigger was obliged to recite over the woman's head on his own until her legs, thighs, torso, and chest had disappeared under the sand. The woman felt she was being throttled, and Nu'man realized that the devils were trying frantically to get out. Then the woman sneezed, and it became clear that the treatment was working according to plan. Next, Isma'il the Gravedigger ordered Nu'man to level the ground around the tomb so that the angels should not be harmed. Nu'man took off his jallabiya so it wouldn't get in his way as he carried out the leveling. His body was pouring sweat and he bent over with the remains of a palm branch to tidy the place as the woman's constricted head beseeched God to grant her recovery. Stillness and a whispering silence buried in the shuddering end of the humid night reigned over the place. Finally, Nu'man sat down next to the woman's head.

The most distressing thing is that the cry from the woman's constricted head did not arise as the result of the bite of a snake or scorpion, or the sudden onslaught of a devil, or a poke from an angel. It was the result of a sharp glance of the eyes at Nu'man's body, the result of which was that the accursed woman awoke to the presence of the topknot rising like a mushroom above Nu'man's head. She asked him—in the midst of her entreaties—about his mother, about his father, and about the sheikh to whom the shaving of his topknot was dedicated. Then, in terrified silence, she turned her head till her weary eyes were able to take in, in the weary dark, Nu'man's thighs, and she whispered, "God forbid, my son, that you be not circumcised!"

The afreets of the place now arose in the darkness and began to wreak havoc on the tomb, for Nu'man had announced that, indeed, he had not been circumcised, that the topknot was linked to the operation of circumcision, and that everyone knew that the topknot was only for those who had not yet been circumcised. The woman's head continued to shiver and shake above the sand, refusing to submit to all the recitations of Isma'il the Gravedigger and his entreaties to the jinn. Then the shuddering overwhelmed the rest of the thrashing body buried in the sands of the tomb until these were thrown out and transformed into a riotous satanic dust and fear seized Nu'man, Isma'il, the rocks, and the palm fronds. There was a first and then a second scream and an eruption of terrible calls for God's help, for it was forbidden for any uncircumcised person to take part in the burying or the filling with sand. The situation became urgent, and Isma'il attempted, with all his strength, to stop the woman from moving, but the devils had opened a fissure in the calm and her body was drawn up out of the enfolding hole—strong, hard, naked, bloody bottomed, and screaming—and the woman, raging, set off immediately along the road. She leaped from the door to the roadway to the grave stones, surmounting barriers, rocks, and the trunks of palms, her deranged voice wrapping the universe, knocking the tops off trees, disturbing the dead in their slumber, and torturing the angels. And sin enveloped Nu'man as he stood there, his mouthing gaping, and tried to cover his body with his hands, while the gravedigger ran first after the leaping, raging woman, then came back to Nu'man, cursing him, kicking him, and striking him on his belly, and the stars coaxed Ursa Major and Ursa Minor into hiding themselves from the devils, and the village slept on, its sleep undisturbed by cry or fear or panic, unwilling to wake for Nu'man or the woman or Isma'il, but for a dog or two which barked briefly, then resumed a listening silence, upon which calm returned and flooded the world, heralding a dawn that seemed likely to be approaching, unconcerned by the confusion that had afflicted us when we discovered that Nu'man—the vehicle for our theory—was hiding from us matters of such sensitivity.

On the Circumcision

erhaps the first to start a serious discussion on the matter of Nu'man's circumcision was a relative on his mother's side who worked as a marketer of hens' eggs in the aftermath of an epidemic that wiped out the area's chickens in the summer of the Coptic year 1668, and who was, or so it is believed, engaged in the preparation of the necessary equipment. Umm Nu'man, however, clarified to her relative the nature of certain impediments that stood in the way of her making the arrangements for her son's circumcision, first that it was conditional upon the slaughter of a kid, second that it required the provision of a white jallabiya and a cap embroidered with gold thread, third her previous and confirmed vow that the circumcision should be carried out on the threshold of the tomb of Sheikh al-Farghal, which was a ride of more than thirty piasters from the village, and finally that she had washed her hands of the fugitive Nu'man, who was, as far as she was concerned, drowned, burned, or dead. Umm Nu'man wept when she reached the last of the impediments to her son's circumcision. Her relative, however, set about systematically demolishing Umm Nu'man's arguments and explained to her that a mother's satisfaction with her child depended on the Lord's satisfaction with the mother, and that the rumors which had circulated concerning what had taken place between Nu'man and the tomb lady was an indicator of God's displeasure with Nu'man, and was based fundamentally on His displeasure with her. Umm Nu'man's heart softened and a disposition to forgiveness appeared in her eyes. Her relative thus turned to the matter of the distance separating the abode of Sheikh al-Farghal from that of Umm Nu'man, stressing with regard to this particular that works are judged by intentions, that religion was sent as a comfort not a curse, and that, as it says in the Qur'an, "only those who are able to undertake the journey" to the tomb are obliged to do so, while at the same time Sheikh al-Farghal, as everyone must be aware, possessed a boundless knowledge of the inner desires of his devotees. Then he launched into the question of what sort of animal should be sacrificed and told stories, received from impeccable authorities, of how Sheikh al-Farghal's acceptance of ex-votos, which at the beginning had been limited to bullocks and camels, had switched, for certain pressing reasons, to chickens and rabbits, and that Sheikh al-Farghal was too large-minded to be angered at his devotees for reductions in their circumstances, the only things required being intention and a noble desire. All that now remained before this surmounter of obstacles was the impediment of the white jallabiya and the cap embroidered with gold thread, which were matters where intentions and noble desires were of no avail, since no barber would apply his razor to the foreskin of a male unless the same were wearing circumcision robes. Umm Nu'man's relative was thus obliged to acknowledge that there was no alternative to the purchase of a white jallabiya and a cap embroidered with gold thread, though he would take it upon himself to come up with another Big Night belonging to any of the sheikhs, whether in the village or some nearby district, on which to perform the ceremony.

The preparations for Nu'man's circumcision were begun immediately following the reconciliation that took place between him and his mother, to which Isma'il the digger of graves, Eid the Barber, and the relative specialized in marketing hens' eggs were party. Umm Nu'man had managed to buy the cloth for the jallabiya and cap from Abd al-Waddud the Nasal, the longest established cloth merchant in the village and its most traditional. Amin the Tailor undertook to make the clothes for a rub' of wheat, and Eid the Barber obtained—with the best of intentions—the ruling needed to allow Nu'man's circumcision to be performed on the threshold of the tomb of the closest sheikh as an alternative to that of Sheikh al-Farghal, who abided at the furthest ends of the earth. Isma'il the Gravedigger made a palm branch with plaited fronds, and also gave Umm Nu'man a quantity of henna from Suez. All of this obliged Umm Nu'man, later, to return to her house in the village, though it had stood empty for six seasons, for removed from the house it would have been impossible for her to circumcise Nu'man, since she needed to be able to prepare the assortment of biscuits, peanuts, and toffees that had to be distributed among the family as a necessary lever by which to obtain from them the cash contributions normally given on these occasions.

After extraordinary efforts and exhilarating arrangements, Umm Nu'man, one midnight, had readied the things necessary for the departure for the tomb of Sheikh Abu Harun in Nazlat Amshul. Eid the Barber and Isma'il the Gravedigger, who had with him a rabbit of large size, rode the jenny of Sheikh Abd al-Aziz Khalil, and Nu'man, with his mother behind him, rode that of Juljula the wife of Tadrus, having placed in front of them the basket of short pastry and biscuits and, even though it was dark, holding aloft the plaited palm branch to mark the occasion. The party traversed fields and deserts until they found themselves, at dawn, looking down on Nazlat Amshul, where the festivities in celebration of Sheikh Abu Harun's birthday were at their feverish pitch.

As soon as they arrived, Isma'il the Gravedigger led the riders through the celebrations, making his way straight to the tomb and trying to avoid the celebrants and God Rememberers, the conjurers and vendors.

Everything was as it should be. Nu'man made a circuit of the candlelit sepulcher, his mother gave some piasters to its servitors and those loitering around it, Eid the Barber spread out a sack, and Umm Nu'man let off a series of ululations that were lost in the racket of the festivities. A rock was called for, Umm Nu'man sprinkled toffees over the people's heads, Isma'il the Gravedigger cut the throat of the rabbit on the threshold, Eid the Barber took out his kit, those specialized in such things fumigated everyone's head with musk and sweet-smelling perfumes, a Qur'an reciter recited something from the Qur'an, and the rays of early morning light flooded the world, at which point a quivering shudder came over Nu'man's face.

The first thing was the shaving—the shaving of the topknot of hair that, for fifteen years, had stood atop Nu'man's pate, inviolate until the redemption of the vow to Sheikh al-Farghal, that sheikh whose abode was so far away that Sheikh Abu Harun had had to stand in for him. With every click of Eid the Barber's clippers over Nu'man's head, the ululations, toffees, and biscuits erupted while the palm branch with its plaited fronds, bespattered with the rabbit's blood, swayed in the arms of Isma'il the Gravedigger, proclaiming joy and happiness. Nu'man wept in the arms of the barber, his mother, overcome with happiness and intoxicated with ecstasy, danced, and Sheikh Abu Harun embraced them all in his protection and benevolence.

Once Eid the Barber had succeeded in removing the topknot and it had fallen onto the laid-out sack, he permitted the celebratory group a moderate amount of time for dancing and ululating. Then he asked Isma'il the Gravedigger to pin Nu'man's arms from behind, and Umm Nu'man's heart was deeply moved as she recalled Abd al-Hafiz Khamis—her husband, her knight, her relative, her man—the one who had departed this life long years ago without it being granted to him to attend the celebration of his son's circumcision. Umm Nu'man therefore wept, her sobs contributing to the clamor the sorrow of a mother and a wife. Eid the Barber shut her up with a few consoling words, after which Isma'il the Gravedigger lifted Nu'man's clothes to his waist and sat him, in his embrace, upon the rock. Umm Nu'man mastered her weeping, converting it into ululations, and resumed her sprinkling of toffees and biscuits over the people's heads.

Nu'man yelled when Isma'il the Gravedigger pinned him from behind, wrapping his arms round his buttocks and his legs round his thighs. Nu'man's limbs appeared to be sleeping, unaware that a deadly assault was about to be unleashed upon them. Eid the Barber read the opening chapter of the Qur'an, the *Everlasting Refuge*, and a prayer to the effect that Sheikh Abu Harun should assume the task of informing Sheikh al-Farghal as to the details of the offering. Then he took out the razor and whetted it at length, Nu'man sitting there the while with his limbs splayed open and his body pinned. Next, Eid's practiced hand reached out to Nu'man's foreskin and the fleshy flexible prepuce was drawn out till it almost came off between the expert barber's fingers. He continued rubbing and then pulling on the foreskin amid the yells of Nu'man, the ululations of his mother, and the joking comments of Isma'il the Gravedigger, and then inserted into Nu'man's member a piece of wood on which to stretch the foreskin, aimed his sharp razor, and cut off the tip, which Umm Nu'man forthwith wrapped in a piece of cloth and held over her head, dancing with it while the blood seeped a crimson red. Next, Eid the Barber's finger returned to the foreskin, only to be forestalled from touching it by a commanding voice that stayed the barber's fingers.

"Whence hails the Master?"

Eid the Barber raised his head, his hands still clutching Nu'man's member.

"From Dayrut al-Sharif. To the day of your own son's circumcision party!"

But the stranger clearly expressed his objection to a barber from another village carrying out a circumcision here and ordered everyone to desist from the operation. Eid the Barber, however, paid no attention to him, demonstrating no more respect for his protest than did Nu'man's thighs. The man was now doubly upset—first owing to the violation of the agreement concluded years before that no barber from another village should trespass upon the local barbers' prerogatives, and second because of the insolence with which he felt Eid the Barber was treating him—and he resumed his yelling once more. Nu'man, therefore, had his circumcision, Umm Nu'man her dancing, and Isma'il the Gravedigger his straining on Nu'man's shoulders halted.

People emerged from the crowd to sympathize, show solidarity with, and support the man's point of view. Isma'il the Gravedigger tried to give the man money, but the situation deteriorated rapidly, for the man refused to allow things to proceed unless a barber from Amshul performed the circumcision. The onlookers showed their secret delight at this development, and the blood flowed copiously between Nu'man's legs, the tip of his foreskin clutched in Umm Nu'man's terrified hand.

Eid the Barber stopped, razor in hand, to explain the circumstances that had led them to overlook this tradition, begging the man to allow him to complete his task and praying that Sheikh Abu Harun (on behalf of Sheikh al-Farghal) should guide and reward him, especially given that the circumcision itself had been performed and all that remained was the cropping. The man, however, remained vociferous in his insistence so that the affair should be a lesson to all inhabitants of Dayrut al-Sharif who did not respect their obligations. Further, he swore a mighty oath that no one should go near the circumcisee and produced a jackknife from his vest and opened its blade.

It appeared, at this point, that things would be difficult to fix. Eid the Barber was furious but powerless to act. Umm Nu'man wavered back and forth between curses and entreaties. Isma'il the Gravedigger tried to calm the man down while other individuals tried to stir him up. Nu'man tried to stand, but felt another savage and powerful flood of pain, and he wept. A peacemaker then appeared and asked Nu'man's family to minimize the damage, respect the oaths that had been taken, and depart.

Eid the Barber turned back to his kit and collected it together, and Isma'il the Gravedigger gathered Nu'man in his arms, lifted him, enveloped in sack, blood, white jallabiya, and gold embroidered cap, and placed him on the jenny, while Umm Nu'man raved on, proclaiming her displeasure at the fabricated fatwa that had substituted a vigorous sheikh like al-Farghal for a feeble sheikh like Abu Harun. Pain wracked Nu'man and a low moan emanated from his mouth and from between his thighs. On the site of the tragedy they left a palm branch with plaited fronds, the skin of a rabbit of large size, broken biscuits, a great deal of blood, and a prepuce wallowing in blood and dust.

On How the Circumcision Was Completed

"All things are in pawn to God's will, and had God wanted Nu'man to be circumcised in Mecca, no impediment could have prevented it, and had He wanted him circumcised in al-Ta'if, nothing could have intervened."

Isma'il the Gravedigger mumbled in confirmation of these cringing consolations that flowed from the mouth the Eid the Barber, the jenny that bore them both lowering its ears and neck until its muzzle was nearly touching the ground. Nu'man, mounted on the jenny following behind, rested his back on his mother's soft chest. The cavalcade proceeded silently and steadfastly, eyes, and thighs, defeated, as Eid the Barber persisted in his attempts to lighten the burden of disgrace caused by Nu'man's incomplete circumcision, expatiating from time to time on his doubts as to the fatwa that had foisted on them the option to change the vow's path from the distant tomb of Sheikh al-Farghal to the nearby tomb of Sheikh Abu Harun. The two donkeys made their way over the violent ups and downs of the area that separates Amshul[1] from their village, stepping over holes and breaks in the road and scaling piles of dirt and the embankments of dykes. From time to time, Eid the Barber would dismount and walk over to Nu'man, who was absent in a trance of pain, to uncover the thing between his thighs and reassure himself. Eid the Barber had succeeded in stopping the blood, twice with coffee grounds and once with smooth dirt, and Isma'il the Gravedigger had been obliged to sing the benefits of coffee grounds and dirt for staunching bloodflow, telling the story of his sister's daughter who had been saved by coffee grounds and only died after envious and ignorant people had misled her family into taking her to the hospital. It was well known that many cases of bleeding had been successfully treated with coffee grounds, chicken dung, dirt from the baking oven, and burned hair, and some of these stories were narrated by Eid the Barber, some by Isma'il the Gravedigger, and some by Umm Nu'man,[2] as Nu'man continued in steadfast silence, limp and prone against his mother's chest, the pain gnawing at him whenever the donkey jumped or stopped or Eid the Barber approached him to reassure himself as to the mess between his thighs. On these occasions, he would scream or moan and then fall silent again, and whenever he screamed or moaned the other riders' feelings of anguish increased—an acute anguish that hung over their heads and shook with the movements of the donkeys, an acute and savage anguish that remained entirely unaffected by those mighty words in which someone attempted to describe the journey of Yusuf the Carpenter, Maryam, and the Messiah from Bethlehem to Upper Egypt.

God always sends men someone to take their hand, rescue them, restore to them their value, wipe the tears from their eyes, expunge the grief from their breasts, and raise their heads until they 'knock against the pride of the angels.'[3]

It was Abd al-Hamid Abd al-Aziz[4] (or his brother Ahmad) who accosted the group at the entrance to their village. At first he inquired about what had happened to them without any clear interest in what that might be. Eid the Barber had barely finished outlining why they had been expelled from the tomb of Sheikh Abu Harun without completing Nu'man's circumcision because they had employed a barber from another village, when Umm Nu'man started wailing, weeping, and howling, at which Nu'man also wept and howled, tears pouring from his eyes and blood from between his thighs, and Isma'il the Gravedigger leaped to Nu'man to uncover what lay between them. The man who had accosted them felt all the pride of the village hemorrhaging over the back of the donkey, soaking Nu'man's clothes and the donkey's coffee-grounds-and-dirt-smeared saddle. The man stepped back, as though so doing would provide him with another perspective from which to view the bloody tragedy, and every time he stepped back, more people gathered and repeated the question; and every time the people repeated the question, one of the members of the mounted group expatiated on the extent of the disaster; and every time one of them expatiated on the extent of the disaster, Umm Nu'man wailed and her tears flowed; and every time her tears flowed, the blood would ooze out in droplets that broke through the dams of coffee grounds and dirt. At this point, and because God does not like anyone to insult the pride of our village, everyone, without exception, agreed that Amshul was a village of evildoers who did not understand the rules and traditions, and observed that Amshul had previously chased one of them from its market, hidden a criminal, cheated a merchant out of his due, sent a bride back without her trousseau, and sold bran cut with dirt. And now this same villainous Amshul wanted to send back one of the sons of Dayrut al-Sharif without completing his circumcision?

Mighty was the stand taken by Abd al-Hamid Abd al-Aziz (or his brother Ahmad), when he swore—in a ringing voice that resounded around the village and disturbed the crows in the fields— to divorce his wife if the circumcision of Nu'man was not completed in Amshul, and declared that, if there were such a thing as a man in Amshul, he should step forth and face them.

Dayrut al-Sharif began to sway, writhe, and cast out into the fields those mighty powers that it kept hidden in the houses, the courtyards, the cafés, the mosques, and the homes of the dancing girls. Its arteries shuddered and convulsed, throwing up out of its belly energies and strengths that bore rifles and knives, hatchets and lances in support of Abd al-Hamid Abd al-Aziz (or his brother Ahmad) and formed a blessed procession to go to Amshul and ensure the completion of the circumcision of its native son, Nu'man, who had awoken to the roaring throngs as they poured in through the heat of the sun and over the mud of the earth. Umm Nu'man ululated, wiping the tears from her eyes, and stretched a loving hand to grasp the donkey's halter and turn it once again in the direction of Amshul, and every head was directed, in pride and determination, toward the heavens as the expeditionary force moved down the long road.

Notable was that day! High the village held its head! Lofty was its pride! A thousand men, it is said, or two thousand, or three, proceeded in that mighty spectacle behind Nu'man's donkey. Discussion and commentary were there none—just the march of zeal and determination, over canals, drains, and the Bahr Yusuf, across farm and field. Eid the Barber hurried over between each leg of the journey to reassure himself as to Nu'man's thighs, while Nu'man followed, with closed, weary eyes, the progress of this doomsday procession, moaning from pain and swooning, and the echoes of the footsteps of the people—unspeaking every one—resounded through the vast spaces of the fields and struck against the distant mountains of the west only to come back to their ears, driving blood, zeal, and determination into their heads. So it was till the outskirts of Amshul, and the tomb of its sheikh Abu Harun, abandoner of Nuʻman, appeared.

At this point, Abd al-Hamid Abd al-Aziz (or his brother Ahmad), their leader, ordered the force to hold up and halt, sent to Amshul to summon its chiefs, and stood, leaning on the back of the jenny of Juljula the wife of Tadrus, on which Nuʻman swayed, his legs limp, cradled in his mother's arms.

We had never realized that our village loved Nuʻman so much. We had never imagined for an instant that this love could be translated, and with such speed, into this host, armed with rifles, sickles, and knives. It was up to Amshul to rethink what it had done. Nuʻman was an orphan, true enough; yet Dayrut al-Sharif was his village, his home, and his father. Nuʻman was poor, true enough; yet Dayrut al-Sharif was his lineage, his strength, and his wealth, and though faced by a thousand villages and a thousand armies, Nuʻman's forces would defeat them all. Nuʻman, while it is true that his eyes were closed, his powers sapped, and he himself spiritless and broken, was still alert, sensing the movement of the people around him and the blood between his thighs, the fellow-feeling, the affection, and the zeal, despite which his veins were not slow to transport amazing quantities of pain from his wound to the inside of his head, causing him to moan and swoon anew.

The chief men of Amshul came. They came quietly, their weapons in their hands, and behind them a long column of the people of Amshul, peering and looking and seeking to understand.

Abd al-Hamid, the leader, was quiet. He greeted the head of the Amshul delegation, took him aside, and explained the matter to him in few words, his sore eyes roving around the army.

The head of the delegation, however, laughed. He laughed till the rifles shook in men's hands and the flowers in the fields. He shook his head with the calm of a man of experience and whispered, "Sheikh Abu Harun and the barbers of Abu Harun are at the service of your son."

At this point, Abd al-Hamid the leader shouted his apology to the people, proclaiming his utter gratitude to Amshul and the men of Amshul, and he swore on the divorce of his wife that there would be no circumcision for Nu'man anywhere but in Dayrut al-Sharif, their mighty village.

The two jennies raised their heads and the army followed behind them. Nu'man fainted, throbbing with pain, silence, and shock. Eid the Barber hurried, between each leg of the journey, to uncover the swelling wound between Nu'man's thighs and bank up the blood with dirt. And Abd al-Hamid, the leader, proceeded at the front of his people, his head held high.

---

1. Amshul is located in the westernmost part of the valley and the distance between it and Dayrut al-Sharif exceeds five hours on a strong, fast donkey, while the common people take twice as long to cover it on foot.

2. The incident of the daughter of the late Sheikh Thabit may be one of those that took place during this period. They married her at nine years of age and she got pregnant when she was ten. She hemorrhaged before giving birth to her child, so for four days running they sought the help of the people who treat hemorrhages with dirt, straw, and scraps of torn-up clothes. Then she was forcibly moved to the hospital in the local town, where she gave up the ghost while the attempts to save her from the results of the rapine and tearing were still ongoing, and her family received her from the hospital in the form of a quantity of scraps of flesh. The strange thing is that the maternal uncle of this victim, who had authority over the family's conduct, was a former principal of the

village school of whom it is said that during one period of his life he composed poetry and was a writer of patriotic songs in support of the struggle against the British.

3. A saying of a blind sheikh, it is not known with absolute certainty what is meant by the expression "He raises their heads until they knock against the pride of the angels," since such sayings only can issue from the mouth of one engaged in a cultural rebellion that has chosen the path of existentialism, and cultural rebellion was a form alien to the society of Nu'man Abd al-Hafiz Khamis.

4. Abd al-Hamid Abd al-Aziz Khalil: one of the common people of the South Side with a predisposition to playing the boss and acting as a leader of men. For some time he was a peasant. Then he became rich through trade and purchased the land of the Ghallab clan. During a period of turbulence, he attained the position of head of the agricultural cooperative. He was a good-natured man who harbored feelings of loyalty to the rich of the village and sought to become closer to them and to enter their world by facilitating their enterprises. He is one of nine in Dayrut al-Sharif who adore such behavior.

On the Days of Might

The thing between Nu'man's thighs swelled and he stayed in the house when in the village, or the hut on the banks of the Bahr Yusuf. Meanwhile events moved quickly and without respite: his mother's things were burgled twice; Sheikh Bakr died immediately after taking his fifth wife and after he had sold his land and his Jeep and spread his mat next to Shahawi the Tomato Seller; weevils destroyed the village's cotton acreage and left the fields as nothing but dry stalks swaying in the autumn wind; in the nearby town Adli Tulba Ulaymi led the student demonstrations calling for the return of Muhammad Naguib; Sheikh Thabit returned to his senses, taking care not to frequent places of ill-repute immediately after the demise of his daughter; Maître Ahmad Abd al-Jawad succeeded in having Ahmad Abd al-Majid, the school principal, seconded to teach in Saudi Arabia; Mahmud Abd al-Latif attempted to kill the leader of the revolution by firing at him in al-Manshiya Square and thereby joined others in a criminal conspiracy whose goal was to create civil strife leading to the overthrow of the regime; Hajja Harlot visited the tomb of the Prophet (blessings and peace be upon him) for the fourth time, and they painted the entrance to her house with lime and pictures; Hajj Hamdan obtained a sentence of sequestration and imprisonment against his best (and sick) friend, Muhammad Mustajab, who thus spent his last months before departing this life under detention in hospital; *Akhbar al-yawm* continued to publish the exploits of Wahid Ra'fat against King Farouk; Sheikh Mahmud Ali divorced his second wife and took back his first; Abd al-Qadir Mursi succeeded in denying his relationship to the Muslim Brotherhood and was released; miracle-working Sheikh Abd al-Jawad died and his disciples set his son upon his throne; the recalcitrant men of the place and its notables announced their abandonment of the Wafd and the Constitutional Liberals and launched preparations to raise the banner of the Liberation Organization; the new teachers' college graduated its first batch of teachers with clean clothes; the House of Awad stirred up some of the common people against the House of al-Gummus, nearly causing a catastrophe; the price of hashish and opium, clover seed and sesame, rose, thus inscribing new names on the lists of the wealthy; Anwar Musa al-Shinnawi closed his primitive clinic in order to join the Salah Abu Sayf theatrical company that had come to the village to film *The Monster*, resulting in the appearance in the daily papers of photos of Anwar Wajdi and Samya Jamal with houses, palm trees, and the men of the village behind them; the government dug up the streets leading to the palaces of the upper class so as to lay pipes for purified water; Hajj Kamil donated a microphone to the mosque of Amir Sinan, which then boomed on for many long nights; the revolutionary government built a community clinic, two schools, and a park in the middle of the village; the Allam Troupe expanded their activities with regard to the setting up of zar groups for the exorcism of the victims of the jinn; the unmarried daughters of the wealthy remained unmarried; Hajja Fiat expanded the number of her houses for the provision of pleasure to those who could afford it; two people were killed in consecutive altercations when the centers for the distribution of American flour were mobbed; Abd Allah al-Ghashim — he of the huge head — got involved in a conflict with his opponents in which he succeeded in splitting several skulls; Sheikh Fu'ad Abd al-Nasir died as the result of a sting from a scorpion that attacked him in the straw store; Hassan Darwish's house collapsed on top of his white, naked daughter while she was taking a bath and she didn't receive a single scratch; Ahmad Abd al-Aziz was transformed into a horseman with a whitish-gray mare on which he trampled the earth, her hoofs stirring up the dust and sending it into people's faces;[1] the schools refused to admit Ramzi Najib, so he spent some time stealing dates and cucumbers until at last a person of means succeeded in having him admitted to a theological seminary, from which he graduated as a priest; Hajja Fatima died for the first time;[2] the first, temporary, constitution of the republican era was issued; an afreet appeared in the tomb of Saint Sarabamwan and another in the area of al-Bughayl; people with big eyes discovered a scandal at the community clinic; the murder of a man in al-Hajjala Road was shrouded in a conspiracy of silence, and was followed by that of Ibrahim Ghalla, of the coppery hair and dented face.

The village swung back and forth, changed, pullulated, and shifted shape, while the victims, the wounded, and the ignorant tottered in its plaza. Nu'man Abd al-Hafiz was swollen between the thighs and Eid the Barber would visit him and try to discover among the pustules some hope of averting the tragedy. When Eid the Barber stopped coming, Umm Nu'man resorted to expert wound curers and spinal-cord cauterizers,[3] but every week that passed the wounds became more inflamed, and Umm Nu'man's conscience and sense of guilt for having abandoned her offering to Sheikh al-Farghal on Sheikh Abu Harun's threshold grew more ulcerated.

People of knowledge placed the quintessence of their experience at Umm Nu'man's disposal: the air of the Bahr Yusuf was said to be poisoned, so Nu'man had to be transferred to the old house in the village; Sheikh al-Farghal was said to be angry, so as conciliation and recompense she put on five dhikr ceremonies that were performed by the cream of the God Rememberers of the area; three successive visits were undertaken to the tomb of the deranged woman who had discovered Nu'man's uncircumcised state in Chapter 6, and during these his mother sprinkled the tomb with salt water in which rasakht granules had been dissolved;[4] Nu'man was transported on the back of a white jenny and given the opportunity of spending the night beneath a sterile male palm tree in whose heart it was believed one of the jinn had taken up residence; the Allam Troupe performed zar ceremonies— three times—and 'set up the bowl' for Nu'man to drive out the evil spirits; the wool of ewes, camel hair, and horse hairs were burned and their ashes plunged into water from an artesian well, and the wound was treated with this potion, despite which it continued to ooze pus, pain, misery, and shame.

Reports differ as to who informed the majestic, and also beautiful, lady of Nu'man's tragedy. Some say that a woman who was envious of Umm Nu'man found consolation for what had happened to him in defaming his reputation. Others that it was a man belonging to the Allam Troupe who informed her. Yet others say that the majestic lady heard the news during a meeting with society's elite in preparation for the convening of the Liberation Organization's first conference in the village square.

It is certain, however, that an order went out from the majestic lady for Nu'man to be brought to her. A constable—who later died, poisoned by ground glass mixed into fish rice—carried him there, and when the majestic lady descended to the square and cast her eyes on Nu'man, Umm Nu'man wept in apology, sorrow, pain, and penitence and kissed her hand, and when the constable raised Nu'man's jallabiya to reveal what was between his thighs, the majestic lady screamed a scream such as she hadn't been heard to scream since the demise of her third, or first, husband and cursed Umm Nu'man, Nu'man, the constable, ignorance, Sheikh al-Farghal, the dust of the tombs, and the Allam Troupe, after which she ordered the constable to rush Nu'man to the big town on the back of the fastest donkey and show him to the doctor there.

It was hot—March, perhaps, or Bashans, or Kiyak—and for the thousandth time Nu'man Abd al-Hafiz was wrapped in a sheet of zardakhan[5] and placed in front of the constable on the back of the jenny of Juljula the wife of Tadrus, with Umm Nu'man hurrying behind them. As the party proceeded across bridges, along the highway, and over canals until it reached the entrance to the town, fire so consumed what was between Nu'man's thighs that he could not even moan.

Things, however, turned out quite differently than we had expected, for a policeman stopped the donkey and prevented it from proceeding along the town streets. After urgings and tears the party was allowed to proceed a few yards, when the policeman stopped the donkey again. Everyone was honking their horns and calling out slogans and screaming and shouting—"Long Live Egypt in Freedom and Independence!" and "Long Live the Liberals!" and "Down with Party-ism!"—and there was no suitable place left for the party to take refuge in. In no time, the marching crowds had surrounded the group and their donkey and started moving it with them and them with it, and a heroic patriot started rebuking the constable, while certain experienced individuals were able to unseat the constable and Nu'man, ordering them to shout slogans and applaud, and one of the cheerleaders was able to stand on the donkey's back and proclaim his noisy happiness at the visit of the great guest. Nu'man was no longer able to move, and his mother, sobbing, put him over her shoulder; a picture appeared in the papers next day with her standing in the midst of the roaring crowds beneath a cloth sign announcing that Dayrut welcomed the Minister of Health.

---

1. We must draw attention here to what happened to the horseman Ahmad Abd al-Aziz, the owner of the gray mare, for a disagreement arose between him and a certain low trader who failed to give the horseman the required salute; Ahmad Abd al-Aziz proceeded to extract the trader's eye, using the blade of his knife; he then paid compensation and spent three years in prison, after which he gave up horsemanship and has never returned to it.

2. Hajja Fatima used to lend money to people for interest and refused to extend a helping hand to any of her children! She fell ill, and they performed the last rites over her after she had bequeathed her wealth to her children. She did not die, however, but lived on in abject poverty as her children refused to give her any aid. She eventually died for the final time.

3. Spinal-cord cauterizers: experts at the cauterization of the coccyx using heated skewers in order to drive out devils and cure fistulas and rheumatism.

4. *Rasakht*: when two pieces of basalt are rubbed together for a long time while being sprinkled with chicory or zinc powder, a red powder results that the common people use, dissolved in water, to treat eye inflammation, wounds, and boils.

5. *Zardakhan*: a type of ticking or linen cloth woven on a loom.

On the Preparations for the Wedding

I must confess that I was taken by surprise when it became clear to me that the idea of Nu'man's getting married did not arise from the days of the inflammation of the thing between his legs. On the contrary, it (the idea of his getting married) was as old as the bruises that covered his knees and the cracks that embellished the soles of his feet. However, "[i]t is always easy for an historian twenty years after an event to see the folly of those involved in it,"[1] and candor compels me to state the outward appearance of the matter while leaving its inner reality to those who like to get to the bottom of things, those who view matters with the eye of the researcher and zealously take their ease by leaning their backs against walls while savoring the warmth of the winter sun or the shade of the end of a summer's day—those capable of understanding, commenting, critiquing, doubting, claiming, complaining, and indulging in mirth. Certain other issues of extreme importance excepted, the idea of Nu'man's getting married while the thing between his legs was being treated with sulfonamide, penicillin,[2] and zinc oxide is to be considered one of the most significant and important of such things.

The degree—and significance—of that importance may be attributed, in our opinion, to the fact that one of the most celebrated of the jinn had declared, while in possession of a woman at one of the regular zar ceremonies, that the thing between Nu'man's legs could only be cured by the righteous mixing of the blood of Nu'man with the blood of a woman whom no male had yet approached, a matter that Umm Nu'man had neglected due to a lack of wherewithal. Subsequently, the matter recurred insistently during the trips that Umm Nu'man undertook from her village to the town in an effort to procure ointments, as when a woman from the Abu al-Uyun family known for the soundness of her judgment and the steadiness of her thinking broached the subject, as did a woman to whom had fallen the lot of trading in the yellow American cheese that was distributed to the masses in those days by the hospitals. After that, it wasn't long before a man who sometimes traded in wormwood and olibanum asserted the appropriateness of this opinion, as a result of which Umm Nu'man announced, as she sat by the open fire, that her son— should he be destined to recover—would be taking in marriage the most beautiful of all the beautiful girls of the village. She then stretched out her hand to where Nu'man sat wrapped in coverings and poured her great tenderness out over his head, causing warmth to rise in the face of the one who lay there submerged in the cold of the month of Tuba.

In matters such as marriage, the sale of farm animals, declarations of the intent to make the pilgrimage to Mecca and the desire to go to town, choice of what to wear, divorce, and the weaning of calves, people think out loud. It follows that those who might be concerned with the business discovered that Nu'man had returned to the land of the living despite his tardy circumcision and the fact that all his

peers—those of them who had survived—had become men
with responsibilities, some of them working in the houses
of the Mu'awada family, some accompanying the animals
grazing in the fields during the boll weevil removal season,
some trading in bran and flour siftings, some stripping
corn cobs or sugarcane stalks or grazing sheep and goats or
running after donkeys transporting manure, none of these
being among those to whom had been granted the ease of life
that comes with owning a piece of land;[3] and behind every
one of Nu'man's peers, behind the walls of the houses, was
concealed a woman with ears of the utmost sensitivity to
every whisper generated by the rustling of the ripe ears of
wheat, the opening of the cotton bolls, the bleating of the
lambs, or the bellowing of the calves, all of which translated
immediately into that mighty desire whose burden all good
men carry before preparing to build a new room on the roof
to serve as a couple's happy home.

At first, the daughter of the son of Abu Abd al-Mawla was
proposed as a bride for Nu'man, but she was rejected because
she spoke through her nose. Then it was the daughter of the
son of Bayyumi al-Banna', but she was rejected because she was
descended from the loins of women known for giving birth to
few male children. Then it was the daughter of the sister of
Abu al-Uyun, but confirmed reports indicated that she was a
good-for-nothing who trembled in front of the baking oven,
as a result of which her bread did not spread properly. Then it
was one of the granddaughters of Kamila, the chicken seller,
and Umm Nu'man was on the point of agreeing and would
have done so were it not for a rumor that she had bad breath.
The lists of candidates included not one possessed of the
qualities needed to gain Nu'man's favor, and Umm Nu'man
felt immense happiness at the difficulty of finding someone

who could rise to the level needed to obtain her agreement. She started to discuss the matter with Nuʻman and, when she sprinkled the mixture between Nuʻman's legs to get rid of the pain and the pus, it was as though she were mixing the zinc and sulfonamide powder with the medicine of great hopes.

As the spathes of the palm trees split and the smell of pollen spread, Abu al-Uyun's sister's daughter began to rise once more to the head of the list; at the same time, the first signs of new skin began to appear on the thing between Nuʻman's legs. The former was, first, because Abu al-Uyun's sister's daughter was the owner, outright, of a ewe and part owner, with a spinster from the West Side, of another. Likewise, people in the know spoke, on numerous occasions and in glowing terms, of how well her bread spread; not to mention that the girl had male siblings and paternal uncles, which reassured everyone as to the likely quality of the offspring. We should not, moreover, ignore what was said of her wisdom, good manners, poise, and attentive listening skills, and of how she avoided joining in with her peers in the secret foolishness that they were accustomed to practice on the shores of Abu Nawa after sunset or during their dealings with the man who maintained the public waterspout. Second, her grandfather, Abu al-Uyun, was among those noted for their taciturnity and for keeping themselves to themselves, with the result that nothing had been heard in his regard that might offend the ear and nothing had been witnessed of him that might hurt the eye. All these were matters that had their weight and might compensate for the reported affliction of the voice of this proposed bride for Nuʻman—the disdained nasality which, or so it was said, prevented her from pronouncing the letter *r* at all.

Envoys began negotiations on the topic, bearing points of view that one would be hard put to reconcile, and the foremost view among those opposed to the project was that of Abu al-Uyun himself, one that he confided to an indiscreet companion and which included his embarrassment at marrying his daughter to a descendant of an abductor of chickens who had squandered a camel—a camel, not a goat—in running after a dancing-girl who was not from those parts. Umm Nu'man was therefore obliged to take the lid off Abu al-Uyun's own scandal, which was that he had twice been caught climbing the wall of a chicken hatchery during the season when the eggs were being hatched and, moreover, that he had performed the heinous act of purloining some of the loaves made for the wedding of Abd al-'Al's son, leaving unsaid the reports that Abu al-Uyun had helped to cover up the disappearance of a lost sheep and that he had given the 'runaways'[4] tips about people's possessions.

However, both the wise and those who harbored good feelings toward the Abd al-Hafiz Khamis and Abu al-Uyun families refused to allow the area of conflict to broaden and slapped the hands of those addicted to entertaining themselves with the bickering of others. Sheikh Husni Abd al-Nazir (whom God rewarded immediately afterward, when he became one of the best muezzins and readers of the Noble Qur'an) confronted Abu al-Uyun at the head of the lane, where he warned him, seriously, against taking pleasure in gossip and clarified for him Nu'man's position in all its aspects—medical, social, and economic. This compelled Abu al-Uyun to reprove Umm Nu'man for spreading tales about him that ought to be considered as consigned to oblivion, if not actually mendacious, and this meant that he was willing to engage in serious dialogue on the matter, which, in turn, meant that he had agreed in principal to become related by marriage to the Abd al-Hafiz Khamis family, given everything that he had heard of their high standards, generosity, and manliness, and meant as well that any subsequent discussions would concern themselves with details and the timetable according to which the first ululation would be launched toward the horizons.

When Nu'man 'stepped out' and left his house on his first trip to visit Abu al-Uyun, he had matured and acquired experience, hardness, and practice. He carried a kerchief that contained rice, two pieces of soap, half an uqqa of peanuts, and a handful of toffees. Some say that he purchased meats for his bride too. What is certain, however, is that his future father-in-law received him welcomingly on market day eve and that he ate a dinner—without seeing his bride—of taro, mutton, and sun-leavened bread and then drank the evening tea in the hall of the house, where he was joined by, among his people, his mother, a relative of his mother's, and two members of his father's family. A discussion was opened in order to fix the bride price. The nishan[5] was left up to Nu'man's family, while the groom's contribution to the bride's dowry was to consist of:

1. Forty pounds, to be paid in its entirety immediately following the winter hold on irrigation, meaning in this case when Umm Nu'man's supply of clamped salted fish had run out.
2. Six kilos of buuya wheat or eight of Australian wheat.
3. Five ratls of clarified buffalo butter or seven of cow's.
4. A goat or a sheep for slaughter.

The two families read the opening chapter of the Qur'an— once so that God might open the path of payment for them, once more to call God's wrath down upon any who might fall short in the fulfillment of his obligations, and a third time to protect the objects of the exercise from illnesses, enemies, fire, poison, envy, and greed. Then everybody laughed and chatted and implored God to cast His blessings over the world.

Over the following months, Umm Nu'man succeeded in arranging the matter of the nishan, whose contents were considered to be a mark of the high regard that the boy felt for his bride; whereas the dowry was a matter that concerned the two families as much as it did the bridal couple, the nishan was the officially sanctioned personal touch.

On the night of the middle day of Sha'ban, Umm Nu'man accompanied—to the sound of ululations—two girls carrying

1. A red shawl in its paper wrapping obtained from Mallawi.
2. A pair of flesh-colored stockings, plus a pair of black stockings for use at funerals.
3. Four pieces of Nablus soap.
4. Four headscarves in four colors, two of them with gold thread and sequins.
5. A pair of slippers with roses on, custom-made in the village.
6. Two pieces of 'Heart's Joy' satin cloth of the most expensive kind.
7. Half a ratl of henna from Suez.
8. Three cones of sugar.
9. Three dye cloths of the sort famous for bringing a rosy hue to the cheeks when rubbed against the skin.
10. Two bottles of Antabli sherbet.

---

1. Miles Copeland, *The Game of Nations*, p. 36.
2. The people of the village prefer to sprinkle onto the wound the powder used for penicillin injections so as to avoid the sting of the needle.

3. There is some exaggeration in this: some of Nu'man's peers entered the rural teachers' school as soon as it was opened in the town and through the efforts of a certain office holder to transfer there a number of the pupils at the elementary school. These members of Nu'man's generation graduated as teachers and were the subject of much attention.

4. The 'runaways': a category of thief living in the desert and the fields, so called because of the belief that they must have run away from the authorities or escaped from prison.

5. The *nishan*: the overture to a life of companionship with the bride. The term is well known in Middle Egypt and the district around the Bahr Yusuf, but I could find no mention of it either in my colleague Zuhayr al-Shayib's translations from the *Déscription de l'Égypte* or in *The Manners and Customs of the Modern Egyptians* by Edward William Lane.

On the Wedding!

As soon as all were assured that the three tail stars of Ursa Major had waned and were no longer in a position to set upon the moon, that the dowry had been paid down to the last item, that Faraj Allah the Tailor had finished mounting the piping on the jallabiya of fresca-cloth, that the month of Tuba had gone, that forty days had passed since the death of one of the bride's relatives, and that it had been ascertained that the dates of the Feminine Impediments were not incompatible with those of the days set aside for the marriage, one of those possessed of wisdom began to guide Nu'man on one of the ways of proving his manhood on the wedding night. A few hours later, the groom's limbs were anointed with henna, and Eid the Barber cropped his hair and his nails and accompanied him to the son of Abd al-Jayyid to obtain an amulet to ensure his sound performance of his duties on that public occasion. After this they went by the tombs of Amir Sinan, al-Khidr, al-Sabbagh, and Abd al-Latif and the little mosque of Sheikh Ali that is on the road to the mill, reading at each the opening chapter of the Qur'an and beseeching each to intercede with God, His messenger, and the people of

His messenger's house, to provide Nu'man with spiritual grace and manhood, and to provide Abu al-'Uyun's sister's daughter with the power of procreation, right living, piety, lack of seductiveness, and right guidance. At this point, it became appropriate for Salma, the best-known woman singer in the village at that period, to make her way to the bride's house and chant:

> *On the brow of the unrobed lad I saw a crescent moon*
> *That cast its light where fields, earth's blessings, and water meet*
> *On the brow of the unrobed lad I saw a cap*
> *With every Abyssinian maid replete.*

The drums rocked to and fro, climbing in the village air and shaking bodies before stoves, baking ovens, and the tethering places of animals, pulling the boys and girls toward the bride's house, while a bass drum, coming toward Umm Nu'man's house, marched in parallel with them. In less time than it takes to perform a prostration in prayer, the men had formed a circle in the street of the Hadayda clan and the ululations spread out from two locations—the house of Umm Nu'man, where the circle of men in its courtyard widened, and the house of Abu al-'Uyun, where women with eyes buried beneath a beautiful heap of kohl, cheeks rubbed with red dill handkerchiefs, and heels chafed with blood-red brick chippings poured forth and joined Salma, she of the mighty throat that had swollen till it hung around her neck as a physical reminder of the thousands of festivities—festivities celebrating the deflowering of brides, circumcisions, verdicts of innocence, releases from prison, the birth of male children, the winning of land cases, the splitting of enemies' bellies, the virtues of those who had died, funerals, and the return of the absent—at which it had sung.

Before the family of Abd al-Hafiz Khamis undertook the journey to the house of Abu al-Uyun, accompanied by the bass drum, they held five rounds of stick-fighting, in which the most creative of their knights—Jad Jayyid Abd al-Nur, Mahmud Abu Dagn, and Abd al-Nazir Ibrahim—took part, as well as some men with only a partial knowledge of stick-fighting—Abd al-Hamid Abd al-Aziz (or his brother Ahmad), someone from the North Side whose name I don't remember, and two men from the villages to the west who had come by coincidence to demand money and stayed to join in the celebration.

Soon the crowds intervened to clear the way for a ululating column of women from the Abu al-Uyun family bearing on their heads the belongings of the bride, which consisted of a mattress, two head pillows, a bolster, a tray of water pitchers, half a qintar of copper vessels, a cupboard with two doors, a green quilt, a basket with her clothes covered with her shawl, and a wooden box, made in Sanabu,[1] decorated with pictures of beautiful birds in two colors, red and yellow, enclosed on all sides within a green border.

No sooner had the bride's things entered Nu'man's house than the old women of the family began to demonstrate their skills at the organization of the bride's bedding arrangements[2] in such a way that no private sounds might escape to the outside; at the same time the men's cavalcade clamored anew as it set off with its drums and pipes to move on—it now being the end of the day—to the bride's family's home to ask permission for her to accompany them to her groom.

Where was Nu'man? Nu'man had bathed early—that is to say in the forenoon—when Eid the Barber performed a final and precision cropping of Nu'man's organs, after which Nu'man, accompanied by an elder of the family, had gone to visit people's homes to invite them to the celebration of his wedding that night and to dinner on the third day. Nu'man was obliged to visit everybody so that no one could reproach him. Afterward, he had to fetch his new clothes from the tailor so that he might appear in all his glory at the end of the day, primped, cropped, and clean.

I don't know whether the proper thing to do is to follow the bride or catch up with the groom. The best thing may be for us to join the crowd of people from the Abd al-Hafiz Khamis family in their slow progress from their own homes to the house of Abu al-Uyun, which they did drumming and ululating, so that to cover a distance that Hajj Zaki Ibrahim— who's lame—covers in the time it takes to drink half a glass of tea it took them the time it would take a waterwheel of limited capacity to irrigate half a faddan, for they would come to a halt every few feet to resume their stick-fighting and dancing, and sing of the virtues of the groom. It might be deduced from this that Nu'man had caused woe to their enemies and grief to the envious for his extraordinary feats as a marksman, a hunter, a dueler with lances, a warrior, a preserver of honor, a protector of orphans, an upholder of truth, and a refuser of submission to injustice, being in these an exemplar of the Abd al-Hafiz Khamis family in general. This done, it seemed good to the people that they should sing of the good qualities of the bride, at which it appeared, without exaggeration, that the bride rivaled the moon in beauty, the sun in heat, butter as far as her saliva was concerned, dough with regard to the pliability of her waist, the gazelle in her gait, the cow in her eyes, the dove in her delicacy, the Night of Destiny in her blessings, the she-camel in her patience, velvet in her fascination, the lotus fruit in the elevation of her nose, the peach in the redness of her cheeks, the Nile perch in the smoothness of her movements, and the cat in her motherliness, being in these things an exemplar of the women of the Abu al-'Uyun family in general.

Few of the brides of our village rode the camel—with its famous howdah—on their journey to the marital home, and rare were they to whom was granted the opportunity of using cars on this occasion. Most of them moved from the houses of their fathers to their new homes on foot, and this was how the daughter of Abu al-Uyun began her eternal journey amid a throng of women, wearing a dress of white satin worked with sequins and gold thread and with, on her head, a red shawl given to her as part of the groom's nishan, and on her feet the slippers with the roses. In front of them all was another crowd, of men, one of whom was carrying an incandescent lamp that they had borrowed from the house of Muhammad Uthman or Mahmud Ali Shinnawi, and which lit up alley after alley and street after street, till it reached that in which Nu'man's family resided. Then, amid an outpouring of ululations, the bride was brought into her new home, taking her first step over the threshold with her right foot. Umm Nu'man washed her in rosewater that she had procured from Abd al-Mun'im the Weaver, whereupon she was carried to Nu'man's room and the door locked, and only the midwife, an old woman from the Abu al-'Uyun family, and Umm Nu'man remained with her. Abd al-Nazir, in all his roughhewnness and with his towering figure, stood in front of the door to stop people from trying to enter. The midwife now started her work. She removed the bride's shawl and certain of her garments that impeded movement and ordered the old woman to take the bride on her lap and wrap her arms under her armpits and around her thighs so that she could not resist. Beneath the bride's naked legs she spread a sack and ordered the man guarding the door to allow the groom to enter.

Nu'man appeared at precisely the right time and forced his way through the throngs of children and women, a cane in his henna-stained hand. The door was opened and then closed, and the men started making a loud noise by beating on it. Nu'man's hand, its finger prepared, reached out and the finger pierced Abu al-Uyun's sister's daughter's locus of virtue. The unsheathed finger penetrated the layer of noble and bloody pain, making the bride scream, but the midwife took note of the groom's dismay, cursed him, took hold of his finger, and repeated the piercing so that the mighty blood flowed, proclaiming the end of the first part of Nu'man's life and giving the signal to the waiting people to fire shots in the air as the bloody handkerchief was thrown over the heads of the crowd, bearing with it the news of the good choice that had been made. After this, everyone moved with Nu'man to the Bahr Yusuf canal, to give the groom the opportunity to cast the seven bricks into the river as happiness enveloped its banks. And at the same time, an ambassador was on the move, approaching the Revolutionary Command Council to deliver to it a strongly worded warning requesting that Jamal Abdel Nasser either withdraw his army from the area around the Suez Canal or permit Britain and France to bomb the country's airports and houses.

---

1. (a) Sanabu, which belongs to the Dayrut tax area, is famous for woodwork, trade in bran, and the manufacture of slippers. (b) No mention is found among the bride's furnishings of a bed or bamboo chairs.
2. Here we must pay tribute to the singular skills of the old women in organizing bedding arrangements for wedding nights, helping women give birth, cutting away afterbirth, and washing and wrapping the dead. Their male peers likewise excel at reaching

into farm animals' uteri to help them give birth, cauterization, the slaughtering of defective beasts, describing the different methods of increasing one's sexual performance, and monitoring the stars.

Modern Arabic Literature

The American University in Cairo Press is the world's leading publisher of Arabic literature in translation.

For a full list of available titles, please go to:

mal.aucpress.com